A Tea Drinker's Novel:
CHILVERTON PARK

Celebrating the Styles of Austen, Trollope & Wodehouse

Susan Russell Thompson

authorHOUSE®

AuthorHouse™
1663 Liberty Drive
Bloomington, IN 47403
www.authorhouse.com
Phone: 1 (800) 839-8640

Published by AuthorHouse 07/11/2016

ISBN: 978-1-5246-1780-6 (sc)
ISBN: 978-1-5246-1778-3 (hc)
ISBN: 978-1-5246-1779-0 (e)

Library of Congress Control Number: 2016911120

Print information available on the last page.

Contents

Chapter 1

At the Adelphi Club, Victorian London

"Wald, old fellow! Where've you been keeping yourself?"

"Wherever I can be assured of not meeting you."

Hastings Bickerstaff threw his head back and laughed heartily. "Wald, you keep me humble, my man."

"I can but try."

"Have a brandy."

"Such was my intent."

The bar at the Adelphi Club was nearly full due to an influx of gentlemen to town for the early part of the Season. The club's membership was mostly younger gentlemen, devotees of the game of Whist and sometimes Loo, though not, as a rule, of the fairer sex. Mr. Erskine Wald, who had wintered in Cannes, had just returned from his recent travels on the continent. Erskine was the only nephew and heir of Sir John Wald of Wald Abbey in Hertfordshire. As such, he was a man of family and some expectations. But, though he was not an intemperate man, he was considered a confirmed bachelor and definitely not a marrying man.

He lounged his tall, thin figure elegantly against the club bar and observed the conduction of a game of Pitch with detachment. His heavy-lidded eyes under thick brows expressed his bemusement while his wide mouth wore its accustomed smile of irony.

Eustace Owerly interrupted his reverie. "Erskine Wald, as I live and breathe!"

"You here?"

"Constantly, my dear. I hear you've been gadding about the continent, scattering largesse at the faro table."

"So I'm told." Erskine shrugged, remembering his mother's lecture of the previous evening.

"It's a shame you missed Lady Fallowell's rout."

"Yes, I'm inconsolable."

"Wasn't the same without you, dear boy."

"I should imagine not."

"That isn't all you missed, Eustace continued. "The Metropolis has been fairly buzzing with activity. Heard about the Tollerson business?"

Brows raised, Erskine Wald sniffed his brandy. "You interest me, my lad."

Hasty Bickerstaff leaned in. "Tollerson's all right."

"Oh, no doubt of it, dear fellow. It's only the suddenness of the break of which I speak."

"With Lady Caroline?" Wald surmised.

Hasty nodded ruefully. "My sister has always been thick with Lady Caroline... practically raised together down at Chilverton, you know. She's certain it was Lady Caroline's decision to break the engagement. Tollerson wasn't pleased, I can tell you. Fairly broken up about it."

"Sad business," drawled Owerly. "They say Lady Caroline wants to turn Roman and join a convent."

"Bosh!" Hasty scowled. "That's hardly probable. Besides, Cecelia would have said."

"Lady Cecelia Stafforth may not know just everything there is to know," sniffed Owerly.

"Nevertheless," Erskine intervened, "I thought the thing was fixed! Whatever was Tollerson about?"

"Nothing whatever! He swears it!" Hasty shook his head. "Apparently Lady Caroline feels that there is not a sufficient agreement of temperament between them."

"Been throwing his weight around, I suppose."

"I can't see it. Tollerson's the coolest fellow going." Hasty puffed his cigar. "I don't understand Lady Caroline. She seems so levelheaded, but she takes odd notions. Tollerson's been damned patient. I don't think I could have stuck it out like he did. She's a deal too flighty for me."

"Lady Caroline flighty?" Erskine's expressive eyebrows shot up again. "That has certainly not been my impression."

He sipped his brandy thoughtfully. "What does her brother say about all this?"

"Birtwood is as fogged as any of us." Hasty shrugged. "But then, he doesn't say much."

"And nor should we, situated as we are here in the bar," Erskine observed. Gentlemen are not accustomed to speak a lady's name in a bar room.

Owerly was piqued. "I just thought you ought to know, seeing how thick you've always been with the family."

"Well, enough has been said about it," Erskine replied. "I shall get to the bottom of this matter myself. It may be well for me to take a little respite in the country for a change of air. Chilverton Park is lovely this time of year. I shall have Mother fix it for me with Lady Sylvia."

Lady Sylvia, Countess of Chilverton, was the wife of the Earl of Chilverton and the mother of Lady Caroline Downey, the lady in question, as well as Hugh Downey, Baron Birtwood. These were the inhabitants of Chilverton Park in Hertfordshire and the first family of the county.

The family at Chilverton Park was well known to Mr. Erskine Wald. While Erskine's father had lived, the Wald's home had been very close to Chilverton Park. Erskine had practically grown up with the children there, as his uncle, Sir John, was a close friend of the Earl of Chilverton. However, in recent years Erskine and his mother, the redoubtable Mrs. Hortensia Wald, had lived in London and had seen comparatively little of the Earl's family. Mrs. Wald was only too glad to arrange a visit to Hertfordshire to see her old friend, Lady Sylvia.

Mrs. Wald took the opportunity to combine the visit with a short stay at Wald Abbey, the old family home, in order to keep in the good graces of the present baronet, Sir John Wald. Sir John had never married and lived alone at the abbey with a set of grizzly servants. His temper was not good in the best of circumstances, but though he did not enjoy company, he insisted on seeing his heir from time to time. Mrs. Wald, who kept a keen eye towards her son's interests, perceived that the time had come due for a propitiatory call on the old bachelor.

Chapter 2

Lady Caroline

Lady Caroline Downey drew a deep breath and lifted her shoulders. The face in her mirror showed a slight blue tint under the eyes. The color in the cheek was almost too heightened, while the rest of the complexion stayed a snowy white. She stared into the dark eyes looking back as if to dare herself. "I will make the effort," she said, determined to appear strong despite feeling a deep internal weakness. Turning for the door, she took a wobbly step and then steadied herself. She lifted her chin and strode to the door.

At the stair she met her father, the affable but elderly Earl of Chilverton.

"How are you, my dear?" asked the Earl.

"Very well, thank you, Papa."

"Glad to hear it, glad to hear it." He gave her his arm. As they entered the drawing room, a rather short, very plump, older woman turned from fussing with some flowers. She squared herself as for battle and stiffened her long upper lip. "Well! I see you have decided to let us see you downstairs this afternoon."

"Yes, Aunt Clara. I am feeling a little better today."

Miss Clara Hilliard gave a huff of derision. "I hope you do not intend to give us one of your little dramas this evening."

"I shall try my best, Aunt."

"As you know, Mrs. Wald is a very old friend of your mother's and mine. I do pray we shall all want to make her stay here pleasant. Let us have no repetition of your performance at dinner yesterday."

Lady Caroline only smiled slightly. It was well known to be fruitless to respond to Miss Hilliard's unpleasantries. "Come and sit with me, Papa," she said, leading him to a small divan by the open windows. "Is Mama annoyed with me?"

"Of course not, my dear! No, no, no! She knows you have your, ahem, difficulties."

"I hope she does know that I try very hard not to cause disruptions. I really do try; its just, sometimes I cannot seem to do all that is expected."

"There now, daughter, do not distress yourself. Have a pleasant evening, and do not be concerned about your aunt. She is just a little anxious about the guests. You know she wants everything to be perfect."

Caroline smiled, remembering her aunt's favorite phrase, "just perfect". If only the dear God would allow perfection in this world, her Aunt Hilliard might be happy. Miss Clara Hilliard, Lady Sylvia, Countess of Chilverton's older sister, was a woman of strong opinions and commanding personality. She had lived with the Earl and his wife since the death of her mother some five years hence. Originally the Earl had thought it probable that the arrangement would be a temporary one. But, old Mrs. Hilliard had not left enough in her estate to make a comfortable home for her daughter in the style to which she had become accustomed. A mild, generous-natured man, the Earl of Chilverton had made his wife's sister welcome in his home despite her occasionally unpleasant behavior and her acerbic criticisms of his daughter, Lady Caroline.

Lady Caroline, in an attempt to calm her aunt's temper, rose and offered to help with the flowers. Miss Hilliard reluctantly accepted the offer with just a tinge of hauteur. She instructed her niece to take particular care with the flowers in order that all should be just perfect for Mrs. Wald's arrival that afternoon.

Chapter 3

Stafforth Hall

At Stafforth Hall, the home of Sir Robert Stafforth in Hertfordshire, very near to Chilverton Park, Lady Cecelia Stafforth arrived home from performing some parish visits to find that she had missed a morning call from the vicar's wife.

"What did Mrs. Pettigrew have to allow?" she asked her sister-in law, the lively Miss Minnie Stafforth.

"Mrs. Pettigrew is a vicious old cow!" Minnie Stafforth set her teacup down with a decided click.

"She's not so old," Lady Cecelia whispered.

Minnie laughed delightedly. "There, you see, Cecilia, you can be as ill-natured as I am."

"Oh, she makes it so hard to be kind," sighed Lady Cecelia.

"My dear, she thinks that as she is the vicar's wife she has the right, nay duty, to interfere in absolutely everything. I've no patience with her!"

"I suppose she thinks Caroline in the wrong."

"She's absolutely furious with her, though of course she wouldn't dream of criticizing."

"My poor Caroline." Lady Cecilia walked to the window. "She's really suffering, Minnie. You must understand that."

"I understand that she suffers, but I will never understand her."

"Minnie, dear, if only you could see how good her heart is. She is sacrificing herself for Lord Charles Tollerson's happiness. It hurts me to hear people say that she is capricious."

Minnie rose and came to her sister's elbow. "Darling, you know that you are the only one who believes in Caroline, and I love you for it. But I think you are far too angelic. I will never know how my reprehensible brother ever had the good fortune to marry you." The sisters kissed fondly. "Now come and have your tea. You'll not help anyone by wasting away."

Lady Imogen Stafforth, Sir Robert's mother, entered with an unusually brisk step. "My dears, I have just had a note from Lady Chilverton. She wishes to see us Monday for luncheon. Mrs. Wald and Mr. Erskine will be down from London. And, we are to have croquet; Mr. Erskine enjoys it so."

"Oh, how nice! Mrs. Wald is such a brick! There's no stopping her."

"Minnie, darling, I wish you would not use such expressions. It sounds so unattractive and no one can tell what you are saying."

"Oh, Mama, you're so old fashioned."

"I daresay, my dear, but I do hope you will not say such things in company."

"Did Lady Chilverton mention any other company?"

"Just the Pettigrews, and young Mr. Felix Parmenter. Quite an intimate group." Lady Cecilia and Minnie exchanged glances.

"Not Lord Edward?"

"Lord Edward will be in town, I am sure, for there's a vote of some sort."

"Tiresome Parliament," sighed Minnie.

"My dear, Lord Edward takes his position in the government quite seriously."

"Yes, I know. It's very inconvenient."

Lord Edward, Viscount Welsey, was the eldest son of the Duke of Bloxham and a member of the House of Lords. His youngest brother, the Honorable Mr. Felix Parmenter, had recently been sent down from college for pranking one of the dons and was in ill favor currently at Bloxham Castle. For some time past, Lord Edward and Miss Minnie Stafforth had been considered almost engaged by their friends. But, of late, Lord Edward had been neglectful, and their relationship was in question. Minnie was growing impatient with Lord Edward's indifference. As Lord Edward's attentions waned, his brother Mr. Felix's interest in Minnie had increased. He had become enamored of the fine blue eyes and silky blond curls of his brother's friend.

Chapter 4

Mrs. Hortensia Wald

As she stepped down from the carriage, Mrs. Hortensia Wald surveyed the Chilverton Park demesne. Sylvia Hilliard, that was, had done very well for herself by marrying the nearly addlepated old Earl of Chilverton. And Clara Hilliard had certainly seized her main chance at proximity to a title, considering her chances of marrying one were questionable at best. She waited for her son's arm before proceeding to the door. "Now, Erskine, you will see a splendid home, and a splendid heiress waiting to be claimed."

Erskine Wald gave his mother a sidelong glance. "I know, Mother, I practically grew up here." He was familiar with his mother's views for him concerning marriage.

"Yes, yes, I know dear. But that has been many years since. Your father's passing has made a difference for us, as you know. Just keep your eyes open. That's all I ask." Erskine shrugged resignedly. He had other intentions for this visit to his old friends. A lady and a friend had by all accounts been cruelly treated by her now-former fiancé. He was determined to see her righted.

Mrs. Wald, a large woman and substantially built, was also a large personality. She possessed strong features, a loud but carefully modulated voice, and a square jaw with a perfectly terrifying smile. She was an acute observer of character and an enthusiastic toady, but generous and good hearted. Her keen, small eyes glinted with intelligence and plenty of life force.

The Walds met Lord and Lady Chilverton in the hall. "Lady Sylvia, I declare! You look younger than ever! And Lord Harold, so pleased! Of course you remember my Erskine. How glorious dear Chilverton is in the Spring! How good of you to have us down to your lovely home. And Clara, my dear, as charming as ever! How this country air agrees with you!"

"Welcome! Welcome!" Miss Hilliard gestured wide. The Earl's eyes turned cold upon Miss Hilliard, a thing that she did not notice, but Mrs. Wald was more observant.

"Lady Sylvia, we are so very obliged to you for this kindness."

"Nonsense, Hortensia! Always glad to have you."

Lady Caroline rose, smiling as Mrs. Wald entered the drawing room. "Lady Caroline, darling girl! How are you, my dear? You are in exquisite looks!"

"Thank you, Mrs. Wald. It is so good to see you again."

"And, I have brought dear Erskine with me, you see."

"Mr. Wald. I am so glad!"

"Lady Caroline. It has been too long."

"Do sit beside me, Mr. Wald. I understand you've been wintering on the continent."

"Yes, I have been at Hyeres and Cannes mostly. Dreadful place, Cannes; one can do nothing but sleep."

"Oh, I have heard you found at least one other occupation," said Lady Caroline, thinking of the Faro tables.

"I am sure you have not been listening to tittle-tattle, Lady Caroline!"

"I have little else to do here at Chilverton, Mr. Wald. Mrs. Pettigrew daily brings us the news."

"Then I understand your plight!"

"Have you seen Hugh in town?" asked Lady Caroline. "He has been little with us here of late."

"Birtwood keeps to his own set, but I've seen him since Christmas. He is burning the candles over his blue books for Lord Attenbury. If I ever talk of taking a ministry position, have me shot at once."

Lady Caroline laughed. "He does seem rather constantly busy. But I do wish he would come home sometimes." She lowered her voice discretely. "It is a bit lonely with just Aunt Hilliard."

Erskine looked toward his mother and saw that she had Miss Hilliard's ear well occupied. "Perhaps I might be pardoned for suggesting that Miss Hilliard's residency here coincides somewhat with Birtwood's prolonged absence."

"I fear you are right," Lady Caroline sighed. "Hugh does not seem to get on very well with Aunt Hilliard."

"Birtwood is a man of fine taste and discretion."

"Oh, Mr. Wald, you are quite wicked!"

"I should certainly hope so."

"What are you saying that is so amusing, Caroline?" demanded Miss Hilliard. "Let us all hear."

"We were just speaking of Hugh, Aunt Clara."

"I did not know that Hugh was so entertaining a subject."

"Oh, Birtwood is a most amusing character, Miss Hilliard," interposed Mr. Wald. "His stories of life at Chilverton are quite diverting."

Miss Hilliard bridled slightly, suspecting herself to be talked of. Mrs. Wald hurriedly reclaimed Miss Hilliard's attention with some current London gossip.

"However do you tolerate it?" whispered Mr. Wald.

"One grows accustomed to it," sighed Lady Caroline.

Having silenced Miss Hilliard, Mr. Wald kept Lady Caroline rapt with his droll stories of Cannes until they all retired for a rest before tea.

Chapter 5

Miss Clara Hilliard

Miss Hilliard did not retire for a rest before tea. Miss Hilliard never required rest. She enjoyed a hearty constitution, for which she was insufficiently thankful to her God as she considered her health due to her own prudence and good sense. She occupied the time on that afternoon before the remaining guests arrived by annoying the maids and the cook, making sure that everything would be just perfect at tea time.

So it was that only Miss Hilliard was present as the guests, the Reverend and Mrs. Pettigrew, arrived. The mild and long-suffering Vicar was left to find occupation with a book while his wife and Miss Hilliard entered conclave on a number of things not their business.

"Has she come down yet?" was Mrs. Pettigrew's first remark.

"She has made an appearance, looking as limp as she can manage." Lady Caroline was seldom given her title or name by the two ladies who referred to her habitually as "she".

"I hear she found herself very ill last night and left the dinner table."

"Nothing but dramatics! She looked as hearty as you or I."

"She seemed very well the day before. She walked all over Chilverborough with my Penelope collecting clothes for the parish schoolchildren."

"She can do everything if she finds it agreeable, but if it's not to her good pleasure, she finds that she is too ill."

"I do not understand why Lady Sylvia allows such capriciousness."

"Sylvia is far too indulgent with her. I have decided that I have no choice but to take the girl in hand myself. She needs correction before she throws her chances away with this senseless behavior."

"I am glad you are here to see the danger, Clara. I have spoken to Lady Sylvia and she just does not respond to my concerns."

Miss Hilliard sighed dramatically. "Sylvia is hopelessly sanguine. She always has been. There is no use trying to show her her duty. But, I thank God I see my duty and I intend to perform it." Miss Hilliard's chin snapped upward as her long lips compressed with determination.

Chapter 6

Tea at Chilverton

Lady Caroline's forehead rested wearily on her palm. "Molly, I don't think I can dress just now," she told her maid. "Would you please bring up some tea?"

"Certainly, Miss. Is it your head again?"

"No. I'm just very tired."

Molly closed the door softly, shaking her head. Caroline rose from the dressing table and moved to the chaise. "Will there ever be an end to this terrible fatigue?" she wondered. A short afternoon rest had left her feeling much worse than tired. There was a sinking feeling in her heart that made her feel it a straining effort to sit upright. "I must go down again," she thought. "The Walds might be affronted if I stay in my room." Tea and a quarter hour's recline on the chaise enabled Lady Caroline to recruit herself for the effort.

Her entrance to the drawing room brought welcoming smiles from her friends, and a "hmph" from Aunt Hilliard. "I'm given to understand that you required to take your tea alone before descending to your family and friends.

Perhaps your mother's Darjeeling is inferior to your taste? You have some special tea, perhaps, that you take in your room, which is more fit for your consumption?"

Lady Caroline gave a slight laugh as if her aunt had said something mildly amusing.

"Dear, sweet Lady Caroline! Do come and sit with me!" Mrs. Wald hurriedly interjected, sitting forward and patting the cushion beside her on the sofa. "My dear, let me hear all your news. I am enchanted with your beautiful new watercolors! Your mother has been showing me all the ones in in this room, and I understand there are many more." Caroline gratefully attended Mrs. Wald. They were pleasantly engaged for a time over a folio of paintings, while Mr. Erskine Wald perched on his elbows on the back of the sofa.

"Charming. Your views are unusual in their intimacy," he observed.

"Yes, I have a limited choice of subject matter and so I narrow my scope, so to speak."

"Excellently done. You create great interest on a small stage."

"Oh dear, you are too kind, Mr. Wald."

"Not at all. However, you can do me a kindness. I would be very gratified if you will show me the location of some of these lovely views."

"They are all right here in our garden."

"Then will you walk out with me, dear Lady Caroline, while the light is soft and the air is mild?" he said with mock formality.

"I shall be delighted, Mr. Wald." Caroline took his offered arm, and they excused themselves from the company.

After visiting a few sites depicted in Lady Caroline's paintings, Erskine noticed a slight breathlessness in his companion and an increased dependency on his arm.

"You are fatigued. Let us rest a while on this inviting bench. My dear, I fear you have not been well." Erskine looked with concern on Caroline's flushed complexion. "It cannot be her heart," he thought. "Her cheeks are as red as this climbing rose."

"Really it is nothing."

"Now, my dear, remember you are talking to your old friend who used to pick daisies for you."

Lady Caroline laughed. "If only those days would come again."

"You have not been happy." Caroline looked down with a slight turn of her head.

"Tollerson should be whipped!"

"Oh, no! No, I understand him completely. I only regret that he does not understand me."

"I knew it must be a misunderstanding. Don't worry, my dear. Tollerson is a pigheaded brute, but I can bring him straight."

"Dear Walders." Lady Caroline used the old, familiar childhood name. "My gallant old friend. Don't tilt at windmills. I'm afraid there can be no reconciliation."

"He's not a windmill. He's a brute. And, I shall tell him so."

Laughing, Lady Caroline shook her head. "It will be no use. After all, he is right. We are not compatible."

"I don't see it. You were made for each other."

Lady Caroline looked down at her hands. "He has given me to understand that he doubts my... my sincerity... my word."

Erskine gaped aghast. "Doubts your word! The filthy cur!"

"I don't mean he thinks me untrue!" she hurriedly clarified. "It's just that he could not give credence..."

"Give credence to what?"

"He cannot understand how I can look so well and still be in such poor health. He believes that the doctors cannot all be mistaken and they can find nothing wrong. Oh Walders! If I only could know what is wrong with me! No one can say what is the matter and yet I cannot do all that is required of me! I just cannot!"

Erskine gently took her hand while she struggled for breath. "Dear Caro. I don't know what is making you ill, but I know you are true. If you say you feel ill, then I know you are ill. Something must be causing it."

"Thank you so much for saying that. I do wish everyone could see that I would take no pleasure in pretending illness."

"I have never known you to pretend anything."

"My dear old Walders. You were ever my good friend."

"And, I always shall be, dear girl. But, my dear, how does the man think that he should be justified in breaking it off with you just because you are feeling unwell?"

"It wasn't he who broke it off," she responded. "I released him because I am unwell."

"At least that prevents the necessity of my removing his teeth and stuffing them down his neck," Erskine muttered. "But, I don't quite understand. You felt that because you are ill you could not marry him?"

Lady Caroline looked earnestly at her friend. "I could not burden the man I love with a wife who is no wife. It isn't fair. All his hopes of marriage and children would be disappointed. I have not the strength for motherhood."

Erskine shook his head. "But, what will you do, Caro?"

"I shall never marry. I shall have my family. There will be Hugh's children someday. That will be enough for me."

Lady Caroline smiled at the look of concern on her friend's face. "Don't worry, dear Walders. It is really all I can envision for the future. My health is so constrained; it is as much as I can manage. Now do let us go in. I should like to sit a while before dinner."

Chapter 7

Hugh, Lord Birtwood

On Sunday, the family was surprised to find the son and heir present on their return from church.

"Birtwood! How good to see you! Why did you not tell us you were coming?"

Hugh, Lord Birtwood, kissed his mother. "Just a flying visit, Mama. I found myself with some time and decided to come down for a day."

"Well!" sniffed Aunt Hilliard. "We should be honored with such a favor!"

"How are you, Aunt? Full of sunshine as usual?" Miss Hilliard huffed in annoyance. Her nephew Hugh had never feared and appeased her as she wished.

Lord Harold leveled a fell gaze at Miss Hilliard as he walked forward to shake hands with his son. "Always delighted to see you, my boy, be it for a day or an hour. Come along to my room while I dress for luncheon." Lord Harold had an idea that his son might have something to discuss and was well aware of his aversion to his aunt's interference. When in the dressing room, Lord Harold dismissed his valet saying that he would only change his coat. Then he turned to his son. "Well, Hugh, it's good to see you. I hope all is well with you."

"Topping, Sir, no troubles in the least."

"Good, good, glad to hear it." Lord Harold hesitated. "I feel that we see you so seldom that I hardly know how you are doing."

"I know, Sir, and I regret it. It is just that it's difficult for me to..."

"What is difficult, son?"

"I'm sorry to say it, Sir, but it doesn't seem like my home anymore. I mean, since Aunt Hilliard took up residence."

Lord Harold turned from his mirror to look in his son's face. "I'm sorry to hear you say so. You know your aunt had no place to turn when your grandmother died. She was quite alone and with barely a competence from the estate."

"I know, Sir, and I think you have been very generous with her. I just thought that someday she would get back on her feet and make a home for herself. She seems to have made herself a fixture here."

"I don't know that she could make an acceptable home with what she was left."

"Not as acceptable as Chilverton, certainly."

"Perhaps that is ungenerous, Hugh."

"I'm sorry, Sir. I don't want to be ungenerous, but neither do I like to see you made use of." Hugh put a hand on his father's arm. "Father, you are the most easy-tempered, unsuspecting fellow going and I have to tell you... you are letting her take advantage."

"I really don't see that I can throw the poor woman onto the streets."

"Of course, but she's not as poor as you think. Did you know that she has had some money from her aunt Harbury who died some three years ago?"

"No, really. I hadn't heard it."

"She has. And I have cause to know that she has invested most of the money from the estate and has done quite well, not to mention the considerable sum she has saved by living on you."

"How do you know all this?"

"Our lawyer happened to mention the money from her aunt. He had no idea that she would keep it secret. And also, her broker belongs to my club. He congratulated me on having such a shrewd investor in the family and I got the rest out of him."

"She has said nothing to me about such investments."

"I daresay not. But now you know it."

"I thought I'd find you here." Lord Birtwood surprised his sister cozied up with a book in a corner of the not much frequented library.

"Hugh, I'm so glad you have come."

Birtwood kissed his sister's forehead. "I see you have the window ajar so as to make good your escape should certain persons come nosing about."

Lady Caroline laughed, "You've found me out!"

Hugh pulled a chair close enough to take Caroline's hand. "How've you been, darling? I hear all sorts of dire stories. Owerly says you've joined a convent."

"Oh, heavens!"

"Really, how are you, my dear?"

"That is a difficult question," Caroline said with a sigh. "I am much as I have been these three years past."

"Not entirely well, in other words."

"I'm afraid not. But, Hugh, I feel less fatigued when you are here, and so much happier. I miss you so. I wish you would come home more often; yet I would fly just the same as you if I could."

"I wish it too, darling. In fact I've just this morning addressed the situation with the governor."

"Do you mean you told him of your differences with Aunt Hilliard?"

"I do indeed, and I think he fully understands me. There are a few things of which I was able to make him aware that may change his disposition towards Auntie Clara."

"If she could hear you call her that!"

"She shall! I shall go this minute and "auntie" her 'til she's purple."

"But what things did you tell Papa?"

Birtwood smiled. "I think I shall just leave you in the dark for a while on that score. It would just make you uncomfortable to know it. I shall tell you later, after the dust settles."

"Oh, how exciting! A dust-up!"

"I certainly hope so. But now, dear girl, for my purpose in coming home just now. I want to understand about this affair with Tollerson."

Lady Caroline blushed. "There is not much to understand... just that Charles is in no way at fault."

"I wish I were sure of that."

"Let me assure you it is so. It was I who broke the engagement."

"But, why, Caro?"

"Dear Hugh. We just spoke of my having been unwell for three years past. Instead of improving, I'm getting steadily worse. There are many days I cannot bear to get out of bed."

"I shouldn't wonder with Aunt Hilliard lying in wait downstairs." Caroline smiled and shook her head. "Darling, Caro. Is it really so bad that you feel you cannot marry? If you really love the man, it seems these things might be overcome."

"When the son of a duke marries, there are more things to consider than love."

"Such as..."

"Such as the continuation of the line. I could not allow myself to be responsible for the extinction of the title."

"You mean that there would be no children."

Lady Caroline nodded. "Charles is an only child; he has no cousins. Were I to marry him, that would be the end of his hopes and his happiness."

"I understand he is rather unhappy now."

"He will recover. Men always do. One day he will be thankful."

Hugh took her hand. "And what of you, darling?"

"I shall be happy in knowing that I have not robbed him of his happiness. I could not have lived with myself had I promised to be his wife when I knew I should not be able to be a wife at all. I shall never marry. I know that I could not undertake the responsibilities of marriage."

Chapter 8

The Croquet Party

Monday, the morning of the croquet party, promised a bright and clement day. Lady Caroline had calculated to a nicety the time that she would find Mr. Wald at the breakfast table. He greeted her with pleasure and drew out a chair for her. "Shall it be ham or bacon this morning?" He served a plate for her. "An uncommon fine day this morning," he observed with uncharacteristic heartiness.

"It is indeed; and so fortunate, for Mama says we're to have croquet today."

"Capital! Croquet is my avocation."

"Mr. Wald, I'm sure you have many more important pursuits."

"None of which I'm aware. May I claim your partnership on the lawn?"

"I should be honored! But you would be missing your chance to have a gossip with Miss Minnie Stafforth. Indeed, I'm not sure that I shan't do her a great disservice to keep you to myself. Mr. Felix Parmenter will be here, but Lord Edward is still in town."

"Ah, Mr. Felix is loosed upon us." Erskine was familiar with Mr. Parmenter's character. "I shall avail myself of Miss Stafforth's company."

"I am quite sure she will be delighted."

Minnie Stafforth tapped her foot with impatience. Of all things, she disliked a fawning admirer. The Hon. Felix Parmenter had strained her temper sadly since the moment she had arrived at Chilverton Park. He was now hopelessly tangling her shawl as he attempted to assist her on with it, an assistance she neither desired nor requested. She flashed a look at her sister, Cecelia, to see if her predicament was observed. Lady Cecelia fully understood the difficulty of Minnie's situation with Mr. Felix. He was brother to the man, who of all men, was Minnie's interest. She naturally wished to be on good terms with all of Lord Edward's family, but Felix was a trial to her. He had conceived a boyish infatuation for her and seemed to be determined to cut his brother out by his assiduous attentions upon her. Lord Edward had been a lethargic lover, seeming to take more interest in his career than in Minnie. It was becoming more than she was prepared to endure.

Lady Cecelia glided to Minnie's side and took her arm. "Come, dear. I want to see Lady Sylvia's roses before we begin our game. You shan't need your shawl; it's quite warm today." Minnie's eyes rolled expressively as they strolled away, leaving Mr. Felix disconsolately holding the discarded shawl.

"Do let me relieve you of that shawl, Mr. Felix," said Lady Caroline, taking pity on his discomfiture. "I hope you enjoy croquet. We are to have a game after luncheon."

"Oh yes, awfully. I hope Miss Stafforth will play."

"I'm sure she will. Mr. Wald has already claimed her as his partner."

"Oh, hang it! I was going to ask her!"

"Never mind, Mr. Felix, the Misses Pettigrew will be here and they are such sweet girls. I am sure you will find one of them a delightful partner."

Felix gave an unconscious shudder. "I'd prefer it if you were to be my partner, Lady Caroline."

"I shan't be playing today, I'm afraid."

"Oh come along! Do play with me. I don't know the Pettigrew girls."

"Come, Mr. Felix, that is hardly gallant! Miss Penelope Pettigrew is a lovely girl. I'm sure you will enjoy her company. Ah, here are the Pettigrews now."

The Reverend and Mrs. Pettigrew, along with their daughters, Fern and Penelope, were frequent visitors at Chilverton. Lord Harold had a fondness for the gentle vicar, and they both shared a penchant for the game of chess. Lady Sylvia had less fondness for the vicar's wife, as she did not care much for parish gossip. But Lady Sylvia's sister Clara was fully absorbed in Mrs. Pettigrew's news so that Lady Sylvia was spared the feigning of interest.

Lady Caroline drew the reluctant Felix to the introductions. Miss Fern Pettigrew was several years older than her sister and also less interested in recreations such as croquet. Penelope, however was of a lively temperament and was delighted to become Mr. Felix's partner for the afternoon. Felix soon found that he had a jolly companion, though he still pined for the loss of Miss Stafforth's company.

Minnie Stafforth prepared to address her croquet ball. "Mr. Erskine, you must not scold me if I miss my wicket. I am not the proficient that you are."

"You simply have not misspent your time on the game as I have."

"I have certainly misspent my time, but not on croquet."

From the ironic tone of Minnie's voice, and her gaze toward Mr. Felix, Erskine deduced that she was referring to her off again lover, Lord Edward Welsey. "Time invested is not time misspent," he offered.

"Ah, but if there is no return on investment?"

Erskine considered a moment. His knowledge of Lord Edward's pursuits and changeable character inclined him to feel that the investment was indeed a poor one. "Then, perhaps, one must stop one's losses."

Minnie reddened slightly but was not offended. "Perhaps one shall," she observed, giving an unnecessarily vigorous whack to her ball. She thought a moment and then ventured, "I wonder if you might be acquainted with Miss Dory Blackwood's brother?"

"George, you mean? Absolutely. Good man."

"He has quite a following in the press, has he not?"

"Phenomenal. I never miss his column."

"He did me the favor to read some of my efforts. He says I have a knack for telling a good story."

"Did he indeed!"

"I'm thinking about submitting a story or two, under a pen name, of course... Montford Styles."

"Absolutely splendid! I will bet you and Mr. Styles will be a tremendous hit. You'll let me know when the stories come out?"

Minnie laughed. "I do have to find a publisher first, Mr. Erskine."

"George can help you there, I'm sure. How does your mother feel about all this?"

Minnie sniffed and assumed a look of determination familiar to her friends. "What Mama does not know cannot trouble her," she observed.

Miss Penelope Pettigrew hit a wobbly shot at Mr. Felix's ball and sent it rolling far enough to give him a poor aspect.

"I say, Miss Penelope, you have no mercy on a poor fellow! Are you quite sure you've never played croquet before this?"

Penelope managed to simper while giggling. "You deserved it for spoiling my shot last wicket."

"I daresay I did." Felix was beginning to feel that Lady Caroline had been right; Miss Penelope made a convivial partner at croquet.

Felix leaned sportively on his croquet mallet. "I say, Miss Penelope, you are jolly good at croquet for a beginner. I'm half tempted to give you the game."

"Oh, Mr. Felix, do go on."

"I've had such a topping afternoon! I think I shall set up a croquet lawn at Bloxham."

"I'm sure you and your friends would enjoy it."

"Actually, I was thinking you might join us for a game." Penelope colored and busied herself with her shot. "My cousin, Tisdale, is down for his sister's wedding next month. I'll see what we can get together then. You would come, wouldn't you, Miss Penelope?"

"I'd have to see if Mama and Papa could spare me."

"Smashing! We'll have ever such fun!"

Chapter 9

On the Terrace

The ladies of the party who were not playing croquet were having tea on the terrace. Lady Caroline had felt the need of her shawl and had excused herself to her room to fetch it. Any slight chill in the air affected her strongly. As she was returning to the party on the terrace, she stopped when she heard her aunt Hilliard's voice.

"She's always dragging that blessed shawl around summer and winter. She'd be warm enough if she would take some exercise and join in the croquet, but I suppose that would be too strenuous for the delicate little thing."

Lady Sylvia stiffened and frowned, but Miss Hilliard was not affected by such signs from her sister.

Mrs. Pettigrew set down her teacup. "I am sorry to see Lady Caroline is not playing with the others. Is she unwell again?"

"She's always unwell, as she says." Miss Hilliard's chin went up, showing her disapproval.

"Who is unwell?" asked Lord Harold as he passed the group unnoticed with his chessboard.

Miss Hilliard felt emboldened by her success with Mrs. Pettigrew. "No one is ill, as we all well know."

"Then why were you saying that someone is unwell. I don't understand."

"Your daughter Caroline is not playing croquet as she says she does not feel 'well enough'." Miss Hilliard allowed her tone to express her disbelief.

"If my daughter says she feels unwell, then we are to understand that she is unwell."

Lady Caroline, who had hesitated to join the group while hearing herself talked of, now came forward and took her father's arm. "Are you having a game of chess with Reverend Pettigrew, Father?"

"What? Yes. In the summerhouse."

"How nice. I suppose he is waiting for you?"

"Yes, yes. I should be getting on." Lord Harold walked on toward the summerhouse and Lady Caroline seated herself beside her mother. Miss Hilliard was sufficiently suppressed by Lord Harold to hold her tongue for the present.

Mrs. Wald, who had been embarrassed for Lady Sylvia during the previous conversation, piped up to dispel the chill. "My dear Lady Sylvia, you have chosen the perfect day for our festivities; such a lovely afternoon!"

"Yes, it is lovely; I am so glad you are enjoying it, Mrs. Wald."

"Perfectly divine! It is such a treat for us, for we must go tomorrow from these beautiful surroundings to my brother, who does not care for outdoor activity."

"Does he not? I am surprised for he has the loveliest view in all the county!" Lady Sylvia exclaimed. "I should be forever out on the terrace of his drawing room if I lived in Wald Abbey."

"Sir John Wald prefers his books, I fear. All that glorious aspect is wasted on him."

"Then you and Mr. Erskine will be leaving us so soon! I am so sorry to lose you!" exclaimed Lady Caroline.

"Bless you, my dear! We will be sorry to leave you, but we mustn't neglect dear Sir John. He has not been well of late."

"Not well?" asked Lady Sylvia. "I hope he is not ill."

"Oh no, not to say ill exactly. He is just slowing down a bit... his age, you know."

"I see. Do give him our regards."

Chapter 10

Miss Hilliard Oversteps

The morning after the croquet party dawned cool and wet. Lady Caroline felt her hands shake as she poured out seed for her canary. She rubbed her hands together. They felt cold and tingled at the fingertips. She wrapped herself in her warmest shawl and called her maid early for tea before sitting down to her devotional book. When Molly came with the tea, Lady Caroline asked that a fire be laid for her. She went down to the guests just an hour before midday. The Walds were preparing to depart for Wald Abbey after luncheon.

Lord Harold stood before the grate in the drawing room wishing there were a fire, though there was only a slight chill. It seemed that his wife never felt the cold as he did.

Lady Caroline, coming down from her room, gave him a kiss. "How are you, Papa?"

"Quite well, my dear. Only a bit chilly."

"I was chilly myself this morning. I asked Molly to lay the fire."

Miss Hilliard drew herself up. "A fire? On a warm morning in May? I should have something to say to you if you were my child!"

"I do have something to say," returned Lord Harold. "That was a capital idea, daughter. Any time you feel chilly, you order a fire. I will not have you cold and uncomfortable."

Caroline kissed him again. "Thank you, Papa." She went to kiss her mother and also her aunt who responded with a sniff.

After luncheon, the Walds made their adieus and departed for the Abbey. "Let us have some coffee," Lady Sylvia suggested. "That should warm you up, Harold."

"Coffee? Excellent idea. Yes, I think I should like some coffee."

Miss Hilliard, who considered coffee unpleasant as well as unhealthful, put her chin up in silence.

"Let me ring, Mama," said Caroline, who was closer to the bell. "I should dearly love a cup of coffee; my hands are tingling as if they were freezing."

"Her hands are tingling," snorted Miss Hilliard. "What? Is this some new symptom of disease come to you? Or, shall I say come to us, for we must all suffer through it."

Lord Harold straightened, not sure he had heard correctly. "Are you suffering from something, Sister? I don't understand you."

Miss Hilliard felt her courage rise with her ill temper. "I only say that we all must suffer these attacks of feigned illness along with Lady Caroline. I should have thought she could give her mother one day of relief from these constant complaints."

Lord Harold turned to face Miss Hilliard fully. "Are you saying, Sister, that my daughter is untruthful when she says she has a complaint?"

Miss Hilliard realized instantly that she had found the end of Lord Harold's tolerance. "No, not untruthful, certainly not. I only say that she imagines herself ill."

"That is not the meaning of feigned. I understood you to say that my daughter feigned her symptoms."

Miss Hilliard, in whose opinion Lord Harold was close to dotting, was overconfident in her ability to talk around him. Still, she decided to backpedal a bit. "Feigned, yes, in that she imagines them."

"I repeat, that is not the meaning of feigned. Do you mean to say that you do not believe my daughter when she says that she is ill?"

Miss Hilliard stubbornly put her chin up. "I mean to say that I do not believe in constant complaint and illness when there is no discernible cause for it."

"I see. That will suffice. Feeling as you do, I can understand that your residence here must be irksome to you. We cannot impose on your patience any longer and will certainly expect you to find a new residence as soon as possible."

"But, Brother..."

"I am aware that it will be no hardship for you presently to provide your own home and am not surprised that you should desire it." Upon that, Lord Harold turned and left the room. Lady Caroline followed him directly.

"Father!"

"Not just now, my dear; I am too warm. But, be assured, I have made up my mind." Caroline, amazed, thought, "Dust up indeed! Whatever did Hugh say to him?"

Chapter 11

Lady Sylvia Intercedes

For some time after Lord Harold left the room, Lady Sylvia and her sister sat silently, looking at the door. Lady Sylvia, knowing her husband to be of an easy temper could not believe her ears. She had seldom seen him so heated. Miss Hilliard was incredulous. Lord Harold had never contradicted her so directly. She was aghast and furious. But in a few moments, it came home to her that she had fatally overplayed her hand. She had been called to account so she did what she always did when caught in her own snares; she burst into tears. "Oh, why does he take me up so abruptly? I did not mean to say Caroline was untruthful. Oh, Sister, surely he cannot mean what he said."

"Clara, I have never heard Harold say anything he did not mean."

"I did not aim to say that he did! But surely he does not intend to turn me out in the street!"

"There, Sister, do not distress yourself. Harold is nothing if not generous and reasonable. I shall go and talk to him. Do calm yourself."

"Go! Talk to him. Tell him I meant nothing unflattering to Lady Caroline in what I said." Lady Sylvia paused and looked with incredulity at her sniffling sister. Sometimes, even though she was her sister, Clara tried her own patience.

Lord Harold was a kind, patient, gentle-tempered man. And, like such men, seldom flew to anger. But, when he became angry, he was not easily moved from it. Lady Sylvia knew that there would be little chance of changing her husband's mind. Still, knowing his generosity, she was confused and dismayed that he had summarily and abruptly turned her sister out of his house. She went to him where he had taken refuge in his study.

"Harold? Dearest... Might I speak with you a moment?"

"Of course, my dear, you may always speak with me."

"Are you feeling quite well? I have never seen you so stern."

"I regret to distress you, Sylvia, but your sister has made herself unwelcome to me."

"But, this is so unexpected. And you know that Clara has no income of her own sufficient to support a home."

"I fear you are mistaken on that point," observed Lord Harold. "Miss Clara Hilliard has been the recipient of a large portion of your aunt Harbury's estate, though she allowed us to believe that Miss Harbury's nephew was the sole heir." Lady Sylvia's face fell in astonishment.

"And, she has invested that money, by all accounts quite astutely, and has been the possessor of a fine income these last two and more years."

Lady Sylvia sat down. "She allowed us to believe..."

"Yes, she allowed us to believe in her own poverty and the nephew's good fortune all this time. I am impressed with the gall of it. And, I tell you, Sylvia, it is time enough. Your sister must find another home."

Chapter 12

Minnie in London

Miss Minnie Stafforth stood at the window of the Stafforth's London home in Bruton Street. "It was so good of Robert to bring us up to town just now."

"Why just now, darling?" Lady Cecelia asked.

Minnie sat close beside her sister. "I will tell you, Cecelia, but it must be our secret... not a word to Mama just yet... or Robert for that matter."

"Such mystery! Whatever is it, my dear?"

"I have come up to town for a particular purpose."

"The Season, one presumes, is your purpose, and a particular Mr. George Blackwood."

"Yes, George has been writing to me, but it's not like that."

"George! It sounds quite like that."

"Oh, George is just a friend! Mr. Blackwood, then if you will have it. He has been helping me to find a publisher for my stories."

Lady Cecelia gasped. "A publisher! Oh, Minnie!"

"Yes Soames & Wrightwell are interested and want to interview me today. I'll need your help to get out of the house without a lot of questions."

"Minnie, your Mama would be so shocked!"

"She needn't know at all... at least for some time. I do intend to use a pen name. If all goes well, then I will make it smooth with her. She's old fashioned, but she's putty in my hands, the sweet old dear."

"Where will you say you are going?"

"I really am going to luncheon with Marie Barnesworth, then I'll hire a taxi to Soames & Wrightwell afterward."

"This is all so exciting! Who would have thought you had all this going on in your head. Minnie, you are too brave!"

"Am I not?"

The Stafforths were still in London when Lady Cecelia and Miss Minnie Stafforth received a call from Lord Edward Welsey. He strolled suavely into the drawing room and shook Lady Cecelia's hand. Greeting Minnie with a confidential smile, he drawled, "Hello, Miss Stafforth. You look charming as always."

"Hello, Lord Edward," she said with dignity. "What a surprise."

"Yes, I am afraid I have been rather occupied. Mr. Peele has indicated that we are to form a new parliament."

"Indeed, that must be good news."

"Yes, I believe it is. I've been asked to fill a new position."

"You are to be congratulated."

"Your congratulations are the most gratifying to me." Lord Edward attempted to look devoted. Minnie looked away.

"But, I have not called to speak of my business..."

"Pray, speak of anything you like."

Lady Cecelia, feeling a little uncomfortable with Minnie's indifference, interjected, "Do tell us of your new appointment, Lord Edward."

"I should not speak of it as a settled thing as yet. Things are still very much up in the air."

"How is your mother? Are we to see her in London this year?"

"My mother is very well, thank you. I do not think she plans to come to town."

Lady Cecelia continued to try to start the conversation among them, but Minnie would not contribute a word, and Lord Edward became more and more unsettled. Finally, he rose to take his leave. "Miss Stafforth, may I hope to see you at Lady Trenewton's ball?"

"I have no plans to attend any balls this year, Lord Edward."

"Well, then, I shall perhaps see you in Hertfordshire."

"Just as you wish, Lord Edward."

Upon his departure, Lady Cecelia turned to her sister. "Minnie, I am surprised at your coldness toward Lord Edward. Has he done anything to displease you?"

"He has done nothing at all; not that he was expected to do anything," said Minnie with great hauteur.

"I see. He has been very busy in Parliament, you know."

"I dare say he has."

Chapter 13

Birtwood Is Engaged

July found Chilverton Park minus one inhabitant. Miss Clara Hilliard, having thought herself grossly insulted by her brother-in-law, had swiftly set about finding herself a modest home in town. Her departure had not been met with great sorrow. Lady Sylvia had become somewhat cool towards her sister when the deception concerning the Harbury inheritance had been revealed.

Lord Harold pottered contentedly into his study for his morning nap. But as soon as he had settled himself comfortably in his chair, the sound of a carriage on the drive disturbed him. Soon, his son Birtwood was with him.

"How are you, Governor? You're looking hearty."

"Fine, my boy, fine. And what brings you home this morning?"

"I've got a bit of news for you and my mother."

"Good news, I hope."

"The best. How would you feel about my getting married?"

"Married? Capital, capital. And who is the girl?"

"I intend to marry Miss Julia Bonneterre."

"Sir Cyril Bonneterre's daughter? That is indeed good news! Your mother will be delighted!"

"I hope so, Sir. Shall we go to her now?"

"Certainly. She is in the morning room, I believe."

Lady Sylvia, who had also heard the carriage arrive, met them anxiously at the door of the morning room. "Hugh! My dear, what brings you here at such an early hour?"

Hugh took his mother by the waist and twirled her around. "Just the best news ever, Mama! Miss Julia Bonneterre has consented to be my wife!"

Lady Sylvia was speechless, but by her astonished smile, Hugh could see that she was well pleased.

Lady Caroline, who was also in the room, ran to her brother and kissed him. "Oh, Hugh! I am so pleased! Miss Bonneterre is the dearest girl in the county."

"So she is, unless it be you, my dear," he said, kissing his sister in return.

The Honorable Felix Parmenter surveyed the newly installed croquet pitch on the lawn at Bloxham Castle with satisfaction. Everything was in readiness for a fine day of sport. Soon the invitations for the croquet party would be going out to family and friends from the pen of his mother, the Duchess of Bloxham. Felix's only concern was how to get Miss Penelope Pettigrew's name onto the invitation list. If he simply asked his mother to invite Penelope, a lot of pointed and uncomfortable questions would ensue, which he was not prepared to answer. Felix sighed and turned his steps towards the tray of decanters that he knew he would find in the smoking room. As he passed through the hall he noted a stack of letters on the table ready for the afternoon post. Among them was one addressed in his mother's hand to his cousin, Miss Eugenia Tisdale. This started a profitable train of thought in Felix's head. The croquet party was to be in honor of Miss Tisdale's coming nuptials and, as the guest of honor, Eugenia would be able to request invitations for a few of her friends. It would be a simple matter to induce his cousin to place Miss Pettigrew among her list of invitees. Felix congratulated himself on his cleverness in solving what had seemed to him to be an insurmountable problem and resumed his course into the smoking room for a celebratory whiskey and soda.

The next afternoon Miss Eugenia Tisdale was surprised to hear that The Hon. Felix Parmenter wished to have a few words with her in the drawing room. Miss Tisdale was not inclined to waste much time away from her wedding preparations for her cousin's concerns. She swept into the drawing room intending to give the impression that she was not at leisure.

"Hello, Felix. To what do I owe the honor of this visit?"

"Hallo, Eugenia. I rather wondered, you know, whether my mother has asked you to submit a list of names to be invited to the croquet party."

"She has, just this morning."

"Good, good, good. That is excellent. I suppose you are going to send her a list of names."

"Felix, I am very busy just now ordering my flowers."

"Yes, yes, I just was hoping you could add a name to your list for me."

"You are wanting me to foist an undesirable guest of yours off on your mother."

"No, no, no! It's just that if I ask mother she will have a lot of unpleasant questions."

"And I'm not expected to ask questions?"

"Miss Penelope Pettigrew is the very respectable daughter of the Vicar of Chilverborough and not in the least undesirable."

"Oh, very well, Felix, I don't have time to argue with you. I shall put your Miss Penelope Pettigrew on my list."

"Thanks awfully, Eugenia. You're topping!"

"I should imagine so."

On the day of the croquet party, the guests were mingling languidly on the lawn under the dappled sunlight. Miss Penelope Pettigrew arrived in her father's carriage and was met promptly by Felix, who steered her quickly away from his mother's view.

"Awfully good of you to come, Miss Pettigrew."

"Oh, Mr. Felix, there are so many people here! I'm afraid I don't know any of your friends."

"Don't worry, Miss Penelope. I'll take care of you. That is, if you'll consent to be my partner at croquet."

"Oh yes, Mr. Felix." The couple made their way to the starting tee. Miss Pettigrew took her shot first, just clearing the first wicket. Mr. Felix grasped his mallet and flexed his arms so that Miss Penelope could admire his fine manly stance. He then gave his ball a mighty wallop, clearing the wicket and the surrounding area of several of the guests' balls. Penelope clapped with glee, considering this a prodigious performance even though her ball had suffered from the proceeding. "Bravo, Mr. Felix!"

"Oh, it's nothing," said Felix. "Just technique. I'll show you some points of the game."

The Duchess of Bloxham found a few moments free from her duties as hostess and strolled along the veranda looking out towards the croquet players. Her eye was caught by the sight of her youngest son with his arms around the waist of an unknown girl while he instructed her on the proper grip of her mallet. A sharp exclamation escaped her lips. "Beatrice!" she called to her daughter. "Who is that girl with Felix? I don't know her."

"I'm afraid I don't know her either, Mama. Perhaps she is one of Eugenia's guests."

"Bring Felix to me at once. I want to speak with him."

Felix looked up in time to see his mother send his sister towards him with an imperious gesture. He grabbed Miss Penelope's hand, causing her to drop her mallet. "We must get away!" he cried and pulled her along down the lawn to a group of guests gathered around the punch bowl. Creeping along behind the guests, he found he was close enough to make a dash for the boxwood border. There they paused long enough for him to peer over the shrubbery and ascertain his sister's whereabouts. Beatrice was standing in the lawn with Penelope's mallet in her hand, scanning the pitch for her errant brother.

"Mr. Felix, why are we running?"

"Because my sister is after... No, no, I just grew tired of the game. I wanted to show you my favorite part of our wood. I do so love a wood, don't you?"

"But you were so abrupt!"

"I am always abrupt. "On the spur of the moment" is my motto. Anything worth doing should be done without delay."

"I suppose so." They acquired the shelter of the wood.

"Let us sit here on this bench and simply enjoy the felicity of being in a wood!" Thus, by moving about the wood from bench to bench Felix was able to enjoy his afternoon with Miss Penelope without maternal interference. He made sure to have moved close to the park gates when the time for her father's carriage to arrive was near. "I say, Miss Penelope, I've had such a smashing afternoon. I hope you have as well."

"Oh I should say so, Mr. Felix."

"Perhaps your mother might not mind if I called sometime at the Rectory?"

"I'm sure she would be happy to see you, Mr. Felix."

Chapter 14

Minnie's Secret Revealed

The most popular collection of short stories in London that Summer came from the pen of Mr. Montford Styles, the celebrated author of "The Wheel of Fashion". Miss Minnie Stafforth, delighted with her success, immediately began work on a novel to be presented in three parts, for which her publisher gave her a small, but respectable advance.

George Blackwood, though Minnie still considered him just a friend, was beginning to feel more than friendship for the quick-witted and intelligent young woman. He had called on her frequently at the house in Bruton Street. But now that Minnie had returned to the country for the winter, determined to complete her novel by spring, George found himself dissatisfied without her lively company. Lady Imogen Stafforth, still unaware of her daughter's literary pursuits, considered George Blackwood to be Minnie's suitor.

"Minnie, my dear, I have a letter from Mr. Blackwood accepting Robert's invitation to come for the shooting." Minnie made a wry face. She wasn't sure that she was pleased to have George around underfoot. She felt quite fond of him, but he was beginning to make more of their friendship than she desired.

"Are you not pleased, dearest?" asked her mother.

"Oh, I suppose its all very well. The shooting will keep him busy."

"I thought you were fond of Mr. Blackwood."

"I am, Mama... just not that tremendously fond."

"But you write to him! I supposed that there was an understanding between you."

"There is a type of understanding. He understands that we are just friends."

"My dear, "just friends" do not write to each other. You are encouraging the young man to think that you are interested in him."

"Not at all, Mama! We just have... information to exchange."

"Information! This is the first I have heard of such a thing. What possible information can you have to exchange with a gentleman? And, for that matter, what is the mysterious occupation that keeps you so busy every day? Does it involve this information which you and Mr. Blackwood exchange?"

Minnie sighed. "Mama, it is nothing."

"Minerva! I insist upon an explanation."

Minnie knew that when her mother used her given name, it was time to tell her all. "I suppose I have kept my secret long enough, Mama. I have been writing a novel."

"A novel!"

"And, Mr. Blackwood is communicating for me with my publisher."

Lady Imogen stared at her daughter, aghast. "In fact, Mama. The novel will not be my first publication. Do you remember "The Wheel of Fashion", which you seemed to enjoy so much? I wrote it."

"But, Mr. Styles..."

"Yes, Mama, I am Montford Styles." Lady Imogen gave a weak exclamation and tottered to a chair. Minnie knelt by her mother's side and took her hand. "Don't be upset, Mama. No one except Mr. Blackwood and Cecelia know that I am the author. Besides, there is no scandal in a lady writing these days. Think of Mrs. Gaskell or Mrs. Oliphant. There are many women writing these days; and very successfully."

"Oh dear, what would your father have said? In my day, it was not done."

"I know, Mama dear, but things have changed. A great many things are done now that were not thought of in your day. Is that not true?"

"Well, yes, dear. Things are not the same. But that does not make them right."

"I'll tell you what we shall do. We shall tell Robert and see what he has to say. After all, he is head of the family now."

"Yes, we must tell Robert, and I am not at all sure he will approve." Minnie felt confidant that, though her brother might not meet her writing with enthusiasm, she could talk him around to taking a more modern view of things than her mother.

Sir Robert Stafforth was a man of his times. He was a tall, confident man, handsome and easy of temperament. His sister Minnie, who was much younger, was always his pet. She approached his study with only a slight flutter of trepidation.

"Robert, I have something I want to tell you."

"Very well, Minnie. Come in. What can I do for you?"

"I have been very busy of late working on something that is very important to me. I have been writing some stories, and I've actually had some success."

"Indeed. What do you mean by success?"

"In August, a small volume of short stories was published under the pen name of Montford Styles called, *The Wheel of Fashion*."

"I believe Cecelia was reading that book."

"I am Montford Styles."

"You, Minnie! How on earth could you know how to find a publisher?"

"That was George... Mr. Blackwood. You know he's a columnist. He is acquainted with all sorts of publishing people and authors and whatnot. That's why I have been writing to him. He has been helping me."

"Has he indeed."

"You're not annoyed about this, are you, Robert? It's all done under a pen name so there is no danger of it becoming known. Besides, plenty of ladies write under their own names these days."

"They are not my sisters."

"Oh, Robert, don't be stuffy about it. This is so important to me! It has given me a new occupation in life. I don't have to sit around waiting for someone like Lord Edward Welsey to take notice of me."

Sir Robert leaned back in his chair and regarded his young sister. "You have no further interest in marriage, then?"

"It's not that."

"Then I should reconsider if I were you. Things are not so different now that young men should not have second thoughts about marriage to an authoress. It would make you positively unattractive to many men. I fear you will not have many suitors."

Minnie flushed slightly and took a deep breath. She knew that her brother was doing her the honor to be quite candid with her. Suddenly she understood another consequence to her new vocation. "Robert, would you and Cecelia mind terribly if I were to live here with you always? I shouldn't want to be in the way. Oh dear, when Papa was alive, I thought of this as my home. I hadn't thought what it would mean to you if I didn't marry."

"Of course this is your home always! I don't believe Cecelia and the girls could do without you. But I would have thought that you would want your own home and your own family. You must give this some hard thought, Minnie. But if you want to continue writing, I have no objection as long as you are not using your own name."

"Oh, thank you, darling Hugh! I really shall think it through, I promise! Now let us see if I can ease Mama's mind." But instead of going directly to her mother, Minnie went straight to her own room. There she curled up in a corner of her couch and set her mind to consider all her brother had said. "Robert is right," she thought. "Men are such cowards. They will all be afraid of me. But I don't think I could tolerate being married to a man so craven as to be afraid of a woman with intellect. Surely someone will come who can value who I am and even enjoy my writing. Does such a man exist?"

Chapter 15

The Shooting Party

The last of November came in cold but sunny, and the hunters were gathering at Stafforth Hall for the partridge shooting. Mr. George Blackwood had arrived the previous evening in time for tea and had found opportunity for only a few words with Miss Minnie Stafforth. George, the youngest son of a baronet, had used his time and education wisely and had made his way into the world of publishing with unusual alacrity. Just out of Oxford, he had been entrusted with a small allowance with which he had kept himself afloat, and in recent years his income from his popular columns had been considerable. He also had had a modest inheritance from his maternal grandfather, which had made him quite comfortable indeed for a literary man. But until he had come to know Minnie Stafforth, he had not considered marriage. He had not reckoned on the power of sparkling eyes and a ready wit. Minnie was different from the insipid girls of his previous experience who seemed reluctant to say anything for themselves.

The first two days of the shooting, George went out with the hunters every day and contented himself with a few words with Minnie over dinner. But on the third day he pleaded a slight headache and stayed behind in the company of the women.

Minnie sat in a chair close to his in the drawing room. "I hope you are not very unwell, George. A headache can be so blinding."

"No really, I'm fine. But I am glad you were concerned."

"That is gallant, Mr. George... wishing a lady to be concerned!"

"No, but I am glad you thought of me."

"If you talk like that I shall go sit with Mama."

"And leave a poor, suffering invalid with no company?"

"Are not the vicar's wife and Lady Cecelia sufficient company for Mr. George Blackwood?"

"Not when Miss Minnie Stafforth is nearby."

"Oh, stop it, you silly man, and tell me what Mr. Soames said about the last chapters I sent."

George settled down to talk business, thinking it better since flirting had not answered. They sat together talking in hushed tones for some time, giving rise to further speculation among the ladies as to their relationship.

That afternoon, George and Minnie walked together down to see the lake. Their conversation moved from literature to the general gossip about town and even a smattering of politics. Minnie, though not previously a student of Parliament, had become interested through reading one of George's serial columns, which had covered the two Houses. George, delighted to talk of one of his primary avocations, was happy to encourage her in her interest.

At dinner, Lady Cecelia had seated Mr. Blackwood next to Minnie, unaware that Minnie had expressed herself uninterested in him. However, Minnie seemed quite happy in his company.

After the shooting ended, the company had broken up and Mr. Blackwood had reluctantly left for London. Minnie found herself discontented. She spent her usual morning at her writing desk looking out the window. For the first time in anyone's memory, she found herself with nothing to say. Finally, she was forced to admit to herself that she missed Mr. Blackwood's conversation. No one else talked to her on such interesting and varied subjects. She mused that it was unfortunate that such a plain man should be the only one with any conversation. George was dark complected and thin compared to Lord Edward, who had the true British fair complexion and the fine leg of a sporting man. Also, George's nose lacked the strong bridge of male beauty, although his eyes, she had to admit, were a melting brown.

Chapter 16

The Duke of Bloxham

The first day of December dawned bright at Bloxham Castle. His Grace, the Duke of Bloxham, who had become irascible of late, strode the length of the drawing room and back several times. His sons, Lord Edward and the Honorables Henry and Felix were all present and quite comfortable except for poor Felix. The Duke stopped his perambulations before Felix and scowled. "Tell me, Sir; what do you propose to live on?" he demanded.

Felix squirmed in his chair. "I thought perhaps you might see your way toward giving me a small increase in my allowance."

"To get married? You, Sir, want an increased allowance in order to marry this girl... this Miss Pettigrew."

"Her father is a gentleman."

"A gentleman, yes. A poor clergyman! You will find yourself without an allowance at all! Your mother will not hear of this."

"If you and the mater would but meet Miss Pettigrew..."

"I have no need to meet the daughter of a parson in the next county."

The Hon. Mr. Henry Parmenter, the Duke's second son, felt the need to interject at this point. "Pettigrew is a good man... solid low church, and his wife is the daughter of Sir Eustace Bowlby." Henry himself was a clergyman, having taken the route of tradition for the middle son. He had gone into the church after university. Presently he was the vicar of a small parish in the next county, a position he had taken while waiting for the parish in his own father's gift to come open.

"Is there any money?" demanded the Duke.

"I believe not," admitted Henry.

"Then I ask again, Sir. What do you propose to live on?" The Duke continued pacing, as he well knew there would be no answer to his question.

Felix, hoping that he would meet with a better reception with his mother, at length found a way to slip himself out of the drawing room in order to seek her in her boudoir. The Duchess of Bloxham was busy at her writing desk with her correspondence.

"Good morning, Mater." Felix went to kiss his mother.

"Felix! It is not often I have the honor of your company in my room."

"I have something I want to say... You know how you've always wanted me to settle down?"

The Duchess set down her pen.

"I'm thinking of getting married, you know, to quite a nice young lady."

"A nice young lady? Who is the girl, Felix?"

"It's Miss Penelope Pettigrew."

"Pettigrew? I do not know any Pettigrews."

"She's the daughter of a gentleman, the vicar of Chilverton parish."

"A clergyman? Felix, you know you must marry money!"

"But, Mater, Penelope is all you could want in a girl. She's pretty and jolly and quite a lady. I'm sure, if you knew her you would love her like a daughter."

"I am sure she will be a lady as she is the daughter of a vicar; but Felix, like her as I might, she must have money for you to live. And what of her family? Do you not wish your children to have the possibility to live as gentlemen?"

"Her mother's father is a baronet."

"Well, that is something, but hardly what you are able to expect. Is there any money?"

"I'm afraid there is not much."

"Felix, you know I cannot approve of such a proposition."

"But Mother, we are engaged."

"I will not hear of this, Felix! The engagement must be nothing."

"But you would not want me to break an engagement?"

"It must be broken! I have nothing more to say on the matter."

Felix left the room discouraged, but not terrifically surprised. He had known that his parents would wish him to find a more eligible girl for his wife. He was also aware that he did not have it in him to make money as some other fellows did. What would they live on if his father did not brass up with the necessary cash? He sighed and sullenly kicked a chair.

Chapter 17

Mr. Blackwood at Chilverton

Lord Hugh Birtwood and Miss Julia Bonneterre were duly married and set happily off to Italy for the honeymoon at the end of March. There had been much excitement for several months at Chilverton over the preparations for the event. Lady Sylvia was happy but exhausted and her daughter, Caroline, was nearly prostrate with a debilitating low fever. Miss Minnie Stafforth had been staying with the family throughout the festivities and now stayed on to be a help to Lady Caroline who had taken to her bed. Minnie could now see at first hand that Lady Caroline was truly ill.

"Minnie, darling, you must not let me keep you. I know you have much to do." Lady Caroline was now in the secret of Minnie's literary undertaking.

"Nonsense, my dear. I can work on my novel right here at your writing table while you rest. Besides, I want to get your opinion of it. I can read you some passages when you feel up to it."

"You are much too good to me, Minnie."

"Just close your eyes and rest while I get my papers and pens. I'll be back in a trice."

Lady Caroline could hardly do other than she was told. She thought much of Minnie's kindness to her and wished that she could think of a way to be a help to her benefactress. She reflected on the things that Minnie had said about Mr. George Blackwood during her stay at Chilverton. Caroline suspected that Minnie cared more about Mr. Blackwood than she allowed. Minnie still insisted that George was just an acquaintance and that she could never feel more for him than friendship. But Caroline had come to know Minnie well enough to perceive that Minnie's independent spirit would hinder her from being able to admit to herself that she really cared for someone. Caroline mused as she drifted off to sleep... how could she bring Minnie and Mr. Blackwood together?

Later that afternoon, Lady Sylvia visited her daughter's room while Minnie took a walk in the garden, her papers carefully hidden under a blotter.

"How are you feeling, my darling? Is your head better?"

"Yes, Mama. Minnie has been reading to me. it keeps my mind occupied, which helps me tremendously."

"I am so glad, dearest. Is there anything I can do for you? Would you care to take some more broth or some biscuits?"

"There is something I would like."

"What is it, my dear?"

"I wish Papa to have some of his literary friends down for a time. Perhaps he could show them his new folios. And among them, have him invite Mr. George Blackwood."

"Is Mr. Blackwood a friend of yours, Caroline? I have never heard you mention him."

"No, Mama, I do not know him, but I wish to have him here for Minnie. I know that Minnie would enjoy his company while she is here tending to me most of the day. They have been friends for some time. I think there is something there."

"Well, dearest, I'll talk with your father and we will see what we can do."

In less than a fortnight, a distinguished gathering of authors and publishers were assembled at Chilverton Park. Among them was Mr. George Blackwood. George had been more than delighted to accept Lady Sylvia's invitation, especially when he knew that Miss Minnie Stafforth was staying at the house. Minnie was surprised and somewhat confused to see George at Chilverton.

"Whatever are you doing here?" she asked him.

"That's a fine welcoming speech, I thank you."

"You know what I mean. I was not aware you even knew Lady Chilverton or the Earl."

"I was invited to meet Sir Quincy Biggs and Mr. Ailwyn Forbes Stalling, the eminent author."

"Oh, I see. You've elevated yourself into quite exalted company. I hope you've brought the latest from Messrs. Soames and Wrightwell?"

"Of course. What do you take me for? I went there directly I knew I was to come here."

"Well then, I suppose you are of some use. What news on the church property bill in parliament? Your last column left it hanging." The conversation took up just as it had left off last November at Stafforth Hall. George was captivated and Minnie, could she admit it, was delighted to see him. They sat heads together for some time in the drawing room.

Lady Sylvia thought to herself, *Caroline is right, there is something there.*

The week passed with Minnie spending the morning writing in Caroline's room, and the afternoon arguing politics with George. Then on an unseasonably warm afternoon of walking and congenial conversation, George decided that he had waited long enough.

"Minnie," he said, "you are a fool about politics, but a decent writer. Why don't we get married?"

Minnie gasped and stared at him in astonishment for several moments. "George," she said, "you are an idiot, a fool, and a pig-headed halfwit. And, yes, I think I will marry you."

Chapter 18

"Dame Margaret of Mayfair"

The end of June saw the return of the honeymooners, Lord Birtwood and his new wife, plus the elopement of another pair of lovers, this time to Scotland. Mr. Felix Parmenter, having seen no other way around his parents' objections, made away with his lady love, Miss Penelope Pettigrew, to the famed destination of Gretna Green, where their marriage was established in the traditional manner by jumping over a broomstick. Afterwards, the newlywed couple sailed as soon as possible for Bruges and traveled thence to Bremerhaven, a remote and inexpensive town in Germany, which possessed a large English community. The Duke of Bloxham railed and threatened and the Duchess wailed and declared herself heartbroken, but still the couple kept to their German refuge and awaited the passing of the storm.

Lord and Lady Hugh Birtwood arrived home from their sojourn in Italy to find their sister, Lady Caroline, much improved. A long period of rest had done a world of good for Lady Caroline, along with the interest she took in the happiness of her friend, Minnie, with her fiancé, George. In addition, the return of her brother and his wife provided her a new interest in life.

During her brother's engagement, Lady Caroline had grown to dearly love her new sister, Julia. Lady Julia was a tall and slender girl with soft brown hair, a lighter color than Caroline's own. Lord Hugh had taught Lady Julia to understand that Caroline was of a delicate constitution and not strong enough for regular exercise. But the weather was so fair and delightful that Lady Caroline could not resist attempting to extend her walks in the garden for longer and longer times. Lady Julia accompanied her, gently encouraging her to rest when she felt weak. The girls became extremely good friends. Lady Julia shared all the excitement of preparing her new apartments in London, and she asked Lady Caroline for her opinion on every color and every fabric she took under consideration. Such excitement and interest had been missing from Lady Caroline's life for a long time. So attached did the young women become that it was a dreadful wrench to Lady Caroline when the newlyweds finally left Chilverton in September for their new London home.

But such was her good fortune that Caroline did not have long to endure in her loneliness. One bright September morning, Miss Minnie Stafforth arrived for a morning call and subsequently stayed on through teatime. She brought with her a bound volume, which she slipped into Caroline's hands privately when Lady Sylvia was out of the room. "It's my novel," she said, *"Dame Margaret of Mayfair."*

"Oh, Minnie! It's here at last! I can't wait to read it."

"You must keep my secret, still. Mama would be so embarrassed if anyone knew that I wrote it."

"I shall be discretion itself. How is the book being received? Have there been a lot of sales?"

"It's early yet for the reviews, but there was a considerable subscription for it."

"How exciting! I do wish I could do something like this to employ my time but I just do not have the talent for it."

"How do you know that unless you have tried? At the very least you could keep a journal of ideas and short sketches. That is how I started to write."

"I have the feeling I should find my head as empty as a jug when I came to try it. But, perhaps I may attempt it. It would occupy one or two unused hours."

"Please promise me that you will try. You needn't show it to anyone, not even to me. But I would love it if you would read some of it to me someday."

"I shall, if I have anything at all to read."

The friends spent a happy afternoon over the book, reading the new bits and talking over the changes to old parts. The hours flew by till teatime when they descended to the drawing room. Lady Sylvia handed a cup of tea to Minnie Stafforth. "Minnie, my dear, have you set a date yet?"

Minnie smiled happily. "Not yet, but I have promised George that I shall make up my mind soon." Minnie did not want to mention that she had been too busy finishing her book and preparing it for publication to spend much time thinking about her wedding. "Dear Robert has been very generous to us and there can be no further reason to wait. What do you think of Christmas and Scotland for the honeymoon?"

"I think that sounds lovely," replied Lady Sylvia. "Will you be ready by then?"

"I think I can manage it. It won't be a large wedding. But perhaps we will wait until March. I just can't decide."

"What does George say?"

"George would marry tomorrow and me without a shift for my back," laughed Minnie.

Chapter 19

Chilverton in Sorrow

As Christmas approached, the excitement over the preparations for the nuptials of Mr. George Blackwood and Miss Minnie Stafforth was interrupted by interest in the return from Germany of The Hon. Mr. Felix Parmenter and his wife, the former Miss Penelope Pettigrew. The Parmenters had been emboldened to return by a letter from the Duchess of Bloxham intimating that all might be forgiven and that the Duke might find himself able to give Felix a small income if the couple would live in England. Both of the young people were delighted to return to England as they had become disenchanted with Bremmerhaven and were happy to escape the hard German winter.

The time soon came for the wedding of Miss Minnie Stafforth and Mr. George Blackwood. Minnie had insisted on the very simplest of church weddings with only the Reverend Pettigrew presiding. The invitation list had been pared down to the bone with only family and the very closest friends attending. Her mother was naturally somewhat disappointed at this but did not impose. After Christmas day the couple made their way to the hills of Scotland to enjoy a chilly honeymoon among the pines.

February, however, found Chilverton Park laden with grief and sorrow... Lord Harold was dead. He had been found one morning in his library, his hands folded quietly on his book, just as if he had drifted off to sleep. The sufferings of the family need not be described. The reader will understand the impact of the death of a well-beloved father and husband. Lady Sylvia's sister, Miss Clara Hilliard, returned to Chilverton in order to support her sister in her grief. To Lady Caroline's surprise and relief, Aunt Hilliard's ministrations proved to be both helpful and considerate. She busied herself with efficacy and made herself indispensable to Lady Sylvia for a time.

Lord Hugh, the new Earl of Chilverton, and his wife did not return to London after the funeral. Eventually Lady Sylvia began to think of relocating to the dower house, Chilverton Cottage, which had been occupied by renters after the death of Lord Harold's mother. Lord Hugh was reluctant to see his mother moved. "There is no need to consider it, Mother. Julia and I have no wish for you to move."

"My darling, I know you do not wish it now, but it will be necessary some day. The dower house is very comfortable. I do not know that I would wish to stay here in this big house now that your father is gone. I feel at loose ends somehow."

"At any rate, I do not want you to think of it for at least a year. We cannot do without you here for a long time to come."

"Well, we shall see. I want you to think more about it though, Hugh. The house will undoubtedly need some repair. It has been rented for a long time."

"That is something we shall look into this summer. Meanwhile, I want you to put it out of your mind completely. This is your home and I want you to feel comfortable here."

Chapter 20

Lady Caroline's Dismay

Gradually, as Winter wore into Spring, it became clear that Aunt Hilliard had no intention of moving back to town. It can be surmised that she felt it her duty to be with her sister, but Lord Hugh suspected that the attractions of Chilverton Park had more to do with it. Lord Hugh was obliged to go to London himself to attend at the House of Lords, so Lady Caroline was left more or less unprotected from her aunt's returning assertiveness. Miss Clara Hilliard considered herself the only person currently capable of running the household. Though Lady Julia was somewhat protected by Miss Hilliard's fear of Lord Hugh, Lady Caroline was not. Aunt Hilliard had always considered her niece to be her own special project, and she intended to mold her to her own specifications.

The dower house renters were moved out and the house was inspected for necessary improvements. Lady Sylvia and her sister were walking through the rooms taking note of what would be needed. Miss Hilliard was focused on making the rooms more elegant. "I should knock down this wall to open up this tiny sitting room. There is no need for this partition here. You will not need a large dining room. And all of these rooms must be painted."

"Everything will be painted, Clara. I don't think I should want this room to be bigger. I like the feeling of intimacy here. And I cannot do without a dining room."

"Nonsense! What company will you have to dinner? Let us look upstairs. These bedrooms are completely inadequate. They must be combined into one room. There is no way you can use either one as they are."

"Then where would Caroline sleep? We shall have to make do."

"I have been meaning to speak with you about Caroline. She should come with me to London. There is no reason for her to stay buried here in the country in these pitiful rooms. Let her come to me. In London I shall be able to keep her active. There will be plenty occupation for her in London to bring her out of her accustomed state of listlessness."

"But I cannot spare Caroline!"

"Think of the two of you confined in this small house after being accustomed to your spacious rooms at Chilverton. Caroline would positively wither and die here without something to bear her up."

"Do you think so, Sister? I could not bear to see her suffer more that she does now. But, oh, how can I do without her?"

"You must think first of your daughter, Sylvia, and do what you must for her sake. Besides, once I have her in London, I can really work on her."

Lady Sylvia was heartbroken to think of losing her daughter's company. She said nothing for the present to anyone about sending Caroline to live in London.

Repairs and improvements went on apace at Chilverton Cottage over the summer months. When it came time to decide about discarding the second bedroom, Lady Sylvia rebelled. She must have the bedroom for Caroline when she would come to visit. She could not face the idea of losing her daughter for too long at a time. "You must allow her to come to me from time to time, Sister, and I must have a place for her." Miss Hilliard was displeased, as she always was when her ideas were not considered to be imperatives, but she conceded. And, as Lord Hugh had returned and was becoming restive, she decided that it was time for her to return to London until Christmas.

The work on Chilverton Cottage was completed and dry by the end of October, but Lord Hugh was still not happy to see his mother move from Chilverton. "Surely you will stay with us until Christmas, Mother."

"Hugh, dear, I shall be not ten minutes walk from you here! We will all be together at Christmas. It is not as if I should be living in the next county."

As the time came for her mother to move to Chilverton Cottage, Lady Caroline prepared to move with her, but it was not to be allowed.

"Caroline, my dear, sit down here beside me. I must speak to you."

"What is it, Mama? You seem very serious."

"I am afraid, as much as it shall grieve me, I shall have to do without you for a while, my love."

"But, whatever can you mean? I am to live with you, am I not?"

"No, my darling, it will be best for you to go to your aunt in London after Christmas and then stay there for the Season."

"Oh, no, Mama!"

"Yes, dear. It will be a wrench to my heart, but I have decided. You are to go. It is not right at your age to be kept always in the country."

"But, Mama, I have no desire to live in London. I have not the spirits for the activities of the Season. I should only be a burden to my aunt, for I am so often ill."

"You will be less often ill with something to occupy you. Your spirits will surely improve with all the entertainments of London at hand. And your aunt desires you to come; indeed it was her suggestion."

Lady Caroline was dismayed almost to tears. "Mama, please do not insist on this. I cannot tell you how much I want to stay at home."

"And I want you to stay too, dear, but I must think of your welfare. I cannot be so selfish as to keep you here. You must go, and that is an end of it."

"Please don't say so, Mama!"

"It is not forever, child. You will come back to visit me from time to time. I have kept a bedroom especially for you. Please, my dear, you must promise to do this, for me."

"I will, if you truly wish it, Mama, but it will be so lonely for me."

"Perhaps it seems so now, Darling, but you will see; the time will fly by for you."

Lady Caroline barely was able to gain her room before bursting into tears. How could she bear to live in London with her Aunt Hilliard? She knew her aunt only kept a civil tongue in her head for fear of Lord Hugh. From Christmas till the end of the Season in August seemed like years to her. She would go to her brother and see if he would intercede for her. She washed her face, straightened her hair, and flew to Lord Hugh's library.

"Hugh! Oh, Hugh, Mama has asked me the most terrible thing!"

"Here! Slow down, Caro. What are you talking of?"

"I am to go to London! To live with Aunt Clara! Oh, Hugh, I cannot do it!"

"Darling. Why cannot you go to London?"

"To live with Aunt Hilliard? Hugh, I cannot think of it with patience!"

Hugh considered. He was not terribly fond of his aunt himself, nor she of him. "What did Mama say?"

"She said it would be good for me to go. She thinks I should not stay always here in the country, but, oh, Hugh, I cannot bear the thought of it."

"Let me speak to her. Perhaps it needn't come to all that. Go back to your room and calm yourself. I shall call for you when I have seen Mama."

Lord Hugh sought his mother in her morning room and Lady Sylvia told him all that she had said to Lady Caroline. He could see his mother's reasons for wishing Caroline to go to town. It would be only for the Season and perhaps the sights and pleasures of London would improve his sister's spirits. He was not sanguine about Caroline's reception of his decision, but he felt she must accede to her mother's wishes.

Lady Caroline was nearly distraught with the prospects that were being prepared for her, but she did her best to control her feelings and prepare herself for the trial. She found some hope in the fact that Aunt Clara had been gentler during the time she had spent at Chilverton after her father's death. Miss Hilliard had moderated her behavior while the house was heavy with grief. And she also had not wished to seem severe in the company of her nephew's wife, lest he hear of it.

Chapter 21

Lady Caroline in London

By Christmas, Lady Sylvia had already completed her move to the dower house while Lady Caroline had remained at Chilverton Park. The family, including Lady Sylvia, was gathered at Chilverton in the drawing room when Miss Hilliard arrived for the holiday. Upon entering the hall, Miss Hilliard tripped up to her niece. "My darling, Caroline... sweet little thing!" She gazed up into Lady Caroline's face adoringly. "How is my girl?"

Lady Caroline kissed the offered cheek and replied, "I am fine, Aunt. I hope you are as well."

"I am in good health as usual, sweet girl." Clara moved to greet her sister. "Sylvia, poor dear, how are you?"

"I'm doing quite well, Sister. So good to see you. How was your journey?"

"Very well, I am always a good traveler." Miss Hilliard prided herself on her robust constitution. She greeted the Earl and Lady Julia and then returned to Lady Caroline and took her arm. "Dear Caroline, I am so pleased that you have decided to come to me for the Season. We shall have such fun!"

"Yes, Aunt Clara." Caroline was familiar with her aunt's incongruous behavior. It was common for Miss Hilliard to gush with affection during the early days of her visits, causing others to drop their guard and run afoul of her. Still it was best to believe in the pleasantness while it lasted.

Miss Hilliard was gay as a lark during dinner. She had evidently set herself on charming Lady Julia as a way to bolster her position with Lord Hugh. All the time of her visit she tried to make herself as agreeable as she could manage to the whole company by making lavishly insincere complements to all. Lord Hugh. who found this behavior more repellent than her usual acerbity, spent most of his time in his library. However, Lady Caroline had no such refuge. Miss Hilliard had decided to devote herself to Lady Caroline and knew no better way to show this devotion than to demand the poor girl's constant company. As the time approached to make their way to London, Lady Caroline was almost relieved. She knew that her aunt's demeanor would change the moment she no longer had an audience. The facade of agreeability was already beginning to show signs of cracking.

The day of their departure arrived. Lady Caroline had been resting as much as she was allowed in order to conserve her strength for the trip. She had packed well ahead of time to make sure of having no last minute rush. When the time came to kiss her fond mother goodbye, she nearly lost her composure but caught herself up immediately. She knew that to show any sign of weakness was like a flag of war to her aunt, so she steeled herself as best she could for the trials to come. Still, she could not prevent one tear from staining her cheek as the last view of Chilverton disappeared behind the trees.

"Let us have no show of sentimentality," warned her aunt. "You are a very fortunate girl to have someone to take an interest in you and to provide you with a home in London with all the luxuries. Any other girl your age would be thrilled and happy."

"I am happy, truly, Aunt. But I shall miss Mama so."

"You will see your mama again soon enough. Let there be no more tears lest I think you are ungrateful."

"Yes, Aunt."

The trip dragged on with Lady Caroline struggling to keep her posture upright as her aunt demanded and not to lean on the seat back. When they reached Miss Hilliard's house in a modestly fashionable street in London, Caroline's carefully conserved strength was nearly gone. "Shall we have a little time to rest before dinner, Aunt Clara?" she asked timidly.

"Rest? Oh, very well if you must. I am over twice your age and I require no rest."

"But, everyone knows of your wonderful constitution, Aunt. You are never tired."

"Well, that is true. Mrs. Pegg will take you to your room and call you in time to dress."

Lady Caroline found that there was no divan in her room on which to rest, only two upright wooden chairs, a table and a bed. Aunt Clara had purposefully chosen the furniture to discourage what she considered to be her niece's idleness. Caroline crawled onto the bed and gave way to her exhaustion. "This is not a very good beginning," she thought.

The months of January and February passed without much difficulty for Lady Caroline. The weather kept the ladies inside most of the time and visitors were few. Caroline was required to sit up late with her aunt, and she was expected to keep her aunt amused with conversation. Unfortunately, Miss Hilliard's idea of good conversation consisted mostly of gossip. Caroline could hardly conceal her dismay at her aunt's spiteful stories about her neighbors and friends. This gave Aunt Clara the impression that Caroline was holding herself aloof and worsened her antagonism toward her niece. But as long as the level of physical activity was low, Lady Caroline was able to satisfy her aunt's demands on her strength, though the long evenings were difficult. It was a relief to Lady Caroline when the weather became less severe and Miss Hilliard's friends began to visit regularly. Still it was difficult to seem not to disapprove of all the disdainful laughter invoked by the continual gossip of the ladies. Then, after the visits were over, Aunt Hilliard would go over the conversations, making unflattering observations about the very ladies with whom she had just shared the gossip. She would chuckle over her own biting remarks and would expect Caroline to join in the derisive merriment.

Still, there was one of Miss Hilliard's friends that Lady Caroline found to be a pleasant companion, a Miss Anna

Cleland. Miss Cleland was a student of literature and could talk with Lady Caroline about the books she was reading. Her visits were very much looked forward to by the lonely Lady Caroline. But her enjoyment of Miss Cleland led Lady Caroline to make a very serious mistake. One dreary morning in March Miss Hilliard announced that she was having a few friends to tea that afternoon. "We'll have Mrs. Wilbur, Miss Simkins and Miss Cleland... just a small group."

"Oh, Miss Cleland is coming? I am so glad!"

"And why should you be so glad that Miss Cleland is coming? What is so very special about Miss Cleland?"

"I just find her easy to talk to, Aunt. We can talk about books, you know."

"Books!" huffed Miss Hilliard. "I know as much about any books as Miss Anna Cleland. You can talk to me about your books." From that day, Miss Cleland was never again invited to tea and her morning calls were avoided with a message that the ladies were out. Lady Caroline was embarrassed at this and crestfallen, but she was soon relieved by an unexpected visit from another quarter. Mr. Erskine Wald called.

Mr. Wald was quite aware of Miss Hilliard's jealous disposition and behaved diplomatically by calling on the aunt with greetings from his mother and spending most of the visit flattering and cajoling Miss Hilliard. Not for a moment was he allowed to speak alone with Lady Caroline but the old friends communicated by little glances and signals that Miss Hilliard could not detect. Mr. Erskine began a habit of calling regularly on the ladies and by his efforts at placating Miss Hilliard he gradually gained her trust and some freedom to speak with Lady Caroline. Finally he judged it to be permissible to ask the ladies to accompany him to a new show of paintings at the London Academy, and he brought his mother to join them. Mrs. Wald was glad to occupy Miss Hilliard while Mr. Erskine stole a little conversation with Lady Caroline. As they stood in front of a singularly unattractive oil depicting Lord Wellington's victory at Waterloo, Mr. Wald ventured to ask Lady Caroline how she had been.

"I have been desolate, Walders, until you came to us. I don't know how I shall survive six more months here."

"I knew it would be terrible for you. How could Hugh have let you go?"

"Hugh and Mama both thought it would be good for me to be in London. Little did they realize how difficult Aunt Clara can be when there is no one to keep her in check."

"We must get you away somehow."

"Oh, how I wish it could be... but how? Mama is convinced I should stay here for the Season."

"Perhaps, if I have your permission, I may talk to your mama about it."

"Yes, but what could you say?"

"I can describe to her how I find you here. That should be enough to bring you home... at the very least for a visit."

"Oh, that would be heaven! How can I thank you, darling Walders?"

"By keeping your chin up till I can manage it. Ah, here is your aunt."

Lady Caroline lived in hope of a visit home until a week later when a note arrived for Miss Hilliard, from Mrs. Wald, informing her that Sir John Wald was now deceased, having suffered a severe attack on his heart. Mr. Erskine and Mrs. Wald would be traveling to Hertfordshire immediately. Lady Caroline was depressed at the news. Erskine would now have no time to carry messages to Chilverton, and her hopes of going home were dashed. A few days later, she worked up the courage to speak to her aunt herself about visiting her mother.

"Visit Chilverton?" exclaimed her aunt. "You have hardly been here three months! But as you bring up the topic, I have been meaning to speak with you about making this your home permanently. I have grown so used to your company that I can hardly imagine doing without you now. What do you think of that?"

"I am honored by your invitation, Aunt, but am I not an expense to you?"

"Oh, that is nothing. You hardly cost me a thing."

"But I could not leave Chilverton. I am much better living in the country. Besides, Mama could not do without me always. She would be so lonely in the house alone."

"I know that your mama can spare you very well for there is excitement enough now at Chilverton. I have had a letter from your mama this morning. She is expecting to be a grandmother in September."

"How wonderful! Oh, how I long to be with them to share their joy! Could I not go to them, just for a time?"

"You do not think of the expense of travel! How am I to afford sending you to Chilverton every few months? We shall both go down for a few days after the child is born."

Chapter 22

The Season

Words could not express Lady Caroline's dismay at the prospect of a permanent residence in London with her aunt. Her friend, Sir Erskine Wald, since he had come into his title, was so harassed by matters concerning his estate that he was unable to return to London to give his assistance. She was quite on her own. She wrote to her mother expressing her desire to return home, but the answer to her letter was not favorable. Lady Sylvia, under the influence of her sister, desired Caroline to stay in London. The Season was just getting underway and she felt that Caroline would settle into London life better without visits home.

Lady Caroline strove hard to resign herself to her situation. It was evident to her that nothing had been said as yet to her mother of her proposed permanent residence with Aunt Hilliard. She could only hope that her mother would not agree when that proposition was made.

One morning Miss Hilliard addressed Lady Caroline while flourishing a letter that she had just received in the morning post. "And now, I have some news for you that I think you will be glad to hear. My very good friend, Lady Culverwell, has written that she will be in town next week with her younger daughter, Miss Cynthia Culverwell. Her eldest is engaged and will not be in town with them. Miss Cynthia will be a very suitable acquaintance for you, my dear."

"That is pleasant news."

"I wish you to be particularly attentive to Lady Culverwell. If she is pleased with you I may persuade her to introduce you at the Marchioness of Trenewton's ball."

"A ball! Oh, Aunt Clara, I could not go to a ball. I have nothing suitable to wear. I have not the spirits to go out."

"Do not worry about what you will wear. I shall take care of that for you."

"But, Aunt, I could not possibly impose on you."

"Nonsense, my dear. All will be done just as it should be. My dressmaker is excellent. I shall enjoy arranging a gown for you. Everything will be just perfect. You will see."

The following week, Miss Hilliard and Lady Caroline made an early call on Lady Frances Culverwell.

"Clara, my dear, how good of you to call so soon."

"I simply had to come as soon as I knew you were in town. I wanted to be the first to welcome our dear Miss Cynthia to the London Season. I know she will be a brilliant success!" Miss Cynthia Culverwell blushed painfully. "And I wished to present my niece, Lady Caroline Downey."

Lady Culverwell looked with interest at Lady Caroline. "Yes, my dear, I remember your mother well. You are very like her." Lady Culverwell introduced her daughter and turned to Miss Hilliard. "She is quite lovely, my dear. Are you going to Amberley?" Amberley was the London home of the Marchioness of Trenewton, whose ball was one of the features of the Season.

"To be quite frank, dear Lady Frances, it has been my hope that you would consider taking Caroline under your wing. It would be such an advantage for her, and I know that her mother would so much appreciate your kindness."

Lady Culverwell considered the proposition. Lady Caroline, had she not been the elder of the two girls, might have outshone the slight, fair-haired Cynthia. Still, Lady Culverwell knew that this would not be Lady Caroline's first Season, and her quiet, unassuming demeanor pleased her. "I shall be glad to take her on. She will be a good companion for my Cynthia."

The girls were talking together quietly on the sofa. Lady Caroline had found that Miss Cynthia Culverwell was somewhat shy. She engaged the young girl with kindly questions and gentle encouragement. Miss Cynthia was immediately taken with Lady Caroline and was thrilled to find that they would attend her first ball together.

The following weeks were taken up in a whirl of dressmaker's appointments and the ordering of gloves. Lady Caroline was frequently taken to call upon Lady Culverwell and Miss Cynthia. Much conversation was made over ribbons and laces, which Lady Caroline loved as much as any girl.

The felicity of this time was interrupted by a call from Mr. & Mrs. Felix Parmenter who were visiting London with Felix's mother. Mrs. Parmenter was very fond of Lady Caroline, who had often made parish calls with her in Chilverborough. The Ladies exchanged embraces and Mr. Felix shook Lady Caroline's hand. "I'm glad to see you well, Lady Caroline. My dear lady wife was concerned about you."

"Concerned about me, but why?"

"I feared that you were ill," said Mrs. Parmenter. "When you did not come to Chilverborough upon your mother's accident..."

"Accident!" interrupted Lady Caroline. "What has happened? Tell me at once!"

"Your mother took a serious fall, I fear, and her ankle was badly injured."

"I am in amazement! No one has informed me of this. She herself has said nothing! Oh, poor Mama! I must go to her instantly!" Then she paused, remembering that she was dependent on her aunt for transportation. She looked earnestly at Mrs. Parmenter. "Oh, Penelope, I am in such a sad state of dependency here."

Penelope Parmenter had had enough experience of Miss Hilliard to understand Lady Caroline's position at once. She turned to her husband. "Felix, my dear, would it not be possible for us to make a short trip to Chilverborough? I have not seen Mama in some time and we could deliver Lady Caroline to Chilverton Park to visit her mother."

"Of course we could, my dear. The mater would not mind."

"Oh, Mr. Parmenter, Penelope, that is exactly what I should wish. I do not think my aunt can have an objection to my going with you. How can I thank you enough for this kindness?" Lady Caroline made her plans with the Parmenters to leave London the next day if at all possible, certain of her Aunt Hilliard's approval. But upon speaking with her aunt when she came back from making a morning call, Caroline found her aunt's attitude to be very different than she had thought.

Miss Hilliard furiously refused to agree to the plan. "How can you think of leaving town just now when I have done everything for you so that you can attend the ball at Amberley? Think of the dress and the crinolines and gloves, not to mention Lady Culverwell's kind consent to present you to Lady Trenewton! You would turn your back on her offer as if it meant nothing. You are a thoughtless, self-willed girl and I have no patience with you!"

"Aunt Clara, surely Lady Culverwell will understand that if my mother is ill..."

"Your mother is not ill. She had a slight fall and is recuperating nicely at Chilverton Park with Lady Julia and all the servants there to look after her. There is no need for you to go and be in the way. Indeed, your mother has asked that I not tell you of her fall specifically because she knew you would want to come home. She does not want you to lose your chance at the finest ball of the Season, nor do I."

"Did Mama really ask you not to tell me?" asked Lady Caroline, bewildered.

"Here. Read for yourself." Miss Hilliard retrieved a letter from her desk and rudely tossed it at Lady Caroline. Caroline read her mother's letter describing her fall and, as Miss Hilliard said, asking that Caroline not be disturbed with the knowledge of it so that she would not miss the great ball.

But Lady Caroline was disturbed. She still felt all the urgency of her wish to see her mother for herself. It was impossible for her to accept that a ball was considered more important than her mother's health. Unfortunately, Miss Hilliard's resistance was unassailable and Caroline was required to write to Mrs. Parmenter and cancel her plan to travel. Her disappointment was severe and she wished to keep to her room to recover her spirits but that was not to be allowed either. She was expected to sit up late with her aunt as usual and talk on indifferent matters as Miss Hilliard saw fit.

Chapter 23

The Ball at Amberley

To Lady Caroline's surprise and delight one morning just before the ball, Sir Erskine Wald was introduced to the drawing room. Miss Hilliard, though she hastened to make a fuss over his new title, eventually left Sir Erskine alone with Lady Caroline. Miss Hilliard well knew that Sir Erskine was not a lady's man and so did not fear to leave him with her niece.

Sir Erskine went to Lady Caroline's side. "Dear Caro, how ever have you been? Have you not suffocated by now?"

"Nearly so," laughed Caroline. "Fortunately, Aunt Hilliard has had the ball at Amberley to keep her mind occupied so I have had a little relief."

"You are going to the ball?"

"Yes, I could not avoid it. But I will have a congenial companion there in Miss Cynthia Culverwell, so it will not be completely without interest. If I could only find a way not to be obliged to dance. I have not the strength for it."

"Perhaps I can be of service there. Let us fill your dance card with my name. We shall stand up once or twice very briefly, then I will monopolize you the rest of the time with my sparkling conversation. I shall be able to ward off any suitors."

"Oh, Sir Erskine, would you? That is so kind of you. But would it not be a terrible bore for you sitting in one place all evening?"

"Balls are a terrible bore. It will give me a good reason to be there. I shall enjoy it. But you shall not call me "Sir" here. Shall I not be your Walders still when we are not in company?"

"Of course, always."

Finally the night of the ball arrived and Lady Culverwell ushered her charges into the grand ballroom. Miss Cynthia was amazed at all the lights and the constant swirl of movement. She stayed close at Lady Caroline's elbow.

"Here is Lady Danforth, girls; let us sit here. Mind your dress, Cynthia."

"Yes, Mama. How many people there are here! I feel I shall be trod upon!"

Lady Caroline looked around anxiously. How would Walders ever find her in this press of people? Finally, she saw his tall, thin form weaving through the crowd, his thick brows lifted in mild amusement. No sight could have been more welcome. She introduced him to Lady Culverwell and he set about charming the older ladies as he was so very accustomed to do. At length he turned to her and asked her to dance. As they approached the dance floor, he said, "How are you holding up under all this heat, my dear?"

"I'm still very well, thank you, but I should not stand up for very long."

"We shall just do a few turns and then sit down again. I like your Lady Culverwell very much."

"She has been a godsend to me. Aunt Hilliard lets me go to her almost daily. And, Miss Cynthia is a dear girl."

"She seems a timid little thing."

"It is her first ball. She's frightened to move. Perhaps you can find someone to ask her to dance?"

"It will be my pleasure." Sir Erskine led Lady Caroline back to her seat where he engaged Miss Cynthia in conversation. Presently he spotted an eligible dance partner and introduced him to Lady Culverwell. Soon Miss Cynthia was whirling about the dance floor with her first partner of the Season.

"Thank you so much, Sir Erskine," said Lady Caroline. "Miss Cynthia was so anxious about being asked to dance and now you have set her at her ease."

"I aim but to serve. However, you seem to have weighty matters on your mind, Lady Caroline. Might I ask if something has disturbed you?"

"It is just something that Aunt Hilliard said to me this evening. It is nothing, really."

"Do tell me."

"She made the observation that I should not expect to attend many more balls at my age, after this Season. She said that I should content myself with the quiet life of a gentlewoman in London."

"She aims to keep you with her! I expected as much. She intends to make you her unpaid companion!"

"She has said before that she wished me to stay with her permanently. She will not even agree to my visiting at home even though Mama has been ill."

"Lady Caroline, this is unacceptable. You cannot allow this to happen."

"I have only one recourse. Aunt Hilliard and I are to visit Chilverton in September. Then I will speak to my mother and ask to stay at home."

Chapter 24

Sir Erskine's Solution

The day after the ball, Sir Erskine called on Miss Hilliard to inquire after Lady Caroline, and found that she was too unwell to come downstairs. Later in the week he called again and found Miss Hilliard out, but Lady Caroline was able to receive him in the drawing room.

"Are you quite recovered from the night of the ball?" he inquired.

"Yes, I am quite well now."

"I am so glad, and I am glad that Miss Hilliard is out; I have something I want to discuss with you."

"What is that?'

"I think something should be done to protect you from a life of servitude with your Aunt Hilliard."

"Oh, if it could be! But what could protect me?"

"I think that we... you and I, should marry."

"My heavens, Walders! But I cannot marry!"

"I remember what you said about Lord Tollerson, how you could be no wife to him. But I do not want a wife in that way. I have never desired to leave an heir. The very thought fills me with terror."

"But why on earth would you want to marry me?"

"I want a home and I want someone to make a home for me. Mother has no idea of leaving London to keep a great empty house in the country for me. And, I want congenial company for when I want to come to that home and leave London behind for a while. What shall I do with Wald Abbey if I do not marry? And how shall I marry if my wife does not understand me? It is just the same as you felt about marrying Tollerson; it would not be fair. And, think of your own position now, with your father gone. Your aunt intends to keep you as her unpaid companion for life. Your mother has not the cunning to oppose her. You know that your aunt can convince your mother of anything she desires. Hugh is busy with his new family. You would feel that you impose there if you asked him to take you in. You might go home for a visit and convince your mother that you should stay, but you know that your aunt will never be satisfied until she obtains her object. She will never leave you in peace... until you are protected by marriage."

"Walders, darling. It seems so odd to marry if we are not in love. I don't know what to think."

"Only think of it, my dear. How many people really marry for love? Do not answer me yet. Give it your consideration for a good long while. You and I, for our own different reasons, are not able to marry in the usual way. But think of the advantages to us both if we do marry.

You will have your own home, not twenty minutes ride from Chilverton. You will not impose on your brother or expose your mother to the machinations of your aunt, and you will escape her servitude forever. It is the only thing for us to do."

When alone, Caroline went into her room and told her maid that she would lie down with a headache. She felt such a whirl of confusion in her mind that she threw herself across her bed. "It is not possible," she told herself. "Is it not wrong to marry where you do not love? But I do love Walders like a brother. Does love not mean more than romantic love? Can it be possible that I should have my own home? But, would it not be wrong?"

By the time her aunt returned home, Lady Caroline did have a headache. Her aunt, who considered that she had given way to Caroline's fancies of illness quite enough since she had allowed her the morning in bed on the day after the ball, became irate. "Tell the girl to get down here," she snapped at the maid. "I have had enough of this nonsense." Miss Hilliard felt herself affronted by her niece's illness. She behaved toward Caroline exactly as if she had offered her insult. Lady Caroline did all she could to be kind to her aunt but was made to feel that nothing was enough. Every sign of Caroline's weakness was cause for fresh affront. Lady Caroline lived under a cloud of disapprobation.

Chapter 25

Minnie Returns to London

The Season wore on into July. Lady Culverwell and her daughter were a great assistance to Lady Caroline. Miss Hilliard was always glad to allow Lady Caroline to go to them. Though the dances and balls of the Season were fatiguing to Lady Caroline, she was glad of them as they provided her some relief from her aunt's ill temper. Sir Erskine continued to call regularly on the ladies but seldom found opportunity to get more than a few words with Lady Caroline.

Late in July, Mr. and Mrs. George Blackwood returned from an extended sojourn on the continent. Minnie Blackwood called on Miss Hilliard and Lady Caroline as soon as she could after arriving in London. Miss Hilliard, who found Minnie irritating, endured her company for a time and then excused herself, leaving the girls alone together. Minnie sat close beside Lady Caroline so that they could talk confidentially.

"Caro, my dear. Are you not wearied to death here?"

"Oh, Minnie, it is so difficult. I do wish I could go home, but Mama thinks it is good for me to stay in London."

"Well, I should disabuse her of that notion immediately!"

"Oh, Minnie. I'm afraid you mustn't say anything to Mama. I fear she would be terribly upset. I intend to get through till August, and then I shall insist on going home."

"As long as you do go home I shan't say anything. But if that old termagant attempts to keep you here as her unpaid servant, I shall have something to say about it."

The visit ended far too soon for Lady Caroline, but she was so buoyed up in spirits afterward that her aunt took notice. "I hope you have not encouraged that young woman to repeat her visit. She is flighty and indelicate in her speech. I do not consider her to be proper company for you."

"I am sorry you think so, Aunt. Mrs. Blackwood has been one of my best friends. Her brother is Sir Robert Stafforth, as you know."

"But she has married beneath herself and disgraced her family."

"You are mistaken, Aunt! Mr. Blackwood is the son of Sir James Blackwood. He is a friend of Sir Robert who has thoroughly countenanced the marriage. Indeed, I believe Minnie's mother was quite pleased with the match."

"Well, some people are easily pleased. I myself should not welcome a newspaperman into my family. If I were your mother, I should forbid you to visit her lest you make the acquaintance of one of her husband's friends."

"I have not yet been invited to visit Mrs. Blackwood, but I hope that you will not forbid her to visit me here. My mother did not object to her staying with me after my father's death."

"Very well, she may visit you here, but I hope it may not be too often," conceded Miss Hilliard.

But it was not a week later that an invitation came for Lady Caroline inviting her to the home of Mr. & Mrs George Blackwood in London for an afternoon reading of some new poems written by one of Lady Caroline's favorite authors. Caroline was delighted but knew immediately there would be trouble. She tried every stratagem to weaken Miss Hilliard's resolve against her attendance. The discussion began to grow somewhat heated on Miss Hilliard's part. She was not inclined to be reasoned out of her own way. Finally Miss Hilliard hit on a stratagem of her own. She put her hand over her heart and abruptly sat down. Two could play at this game of feigning illness to get one's way. "There, you impertinent girl; I suppose this is what you were wanting."

"What's the matter, Aunt Clara? Are you unwell?"

"It's my heart again. Ring for Mrs. Pegg immediately!"

Caroline ran breathlessly to bring the housekeeper. "Something is amiss with my Aunt and she needs your assistance! She says it is her heart!" Mrs. Pegg lifted her eyebrows but wisely said nothing.

"Pegg, fetch my pills; the blue ones!" Pegg looked amazed. "Oh, never mind. Just help me upstairs." Caroline and Mrs. Pegg each took an arm and helped Miss Hilliard to her room where she collapsed with loud sighs upon the bed.

"Aunt Clara, I will call for the doctor at once!"

"No, no, there is no need for that as yet. Just let me take my pills and I will recover as long as there is no further fuss to make my heart beat so."

"Where are your pills?"

"Right here in the nightstand." She indicated a packet of blue pills, which she normally took for stomach distress. "Bring me some water!" She swallowed two large pills and lay back panting on her pillow. "Now leave me. I need rest."

Lady Caroline and Mrs. Pegg left the room quietly. Pegg shook her head in bewilderment but Caroline was not sure what that sign was to mean. "Mrs. Pegg, I did not know that my Aunt was troubled with her heart."

"No, My Lady," said Pegg noncommittally.

"It seemed to come on so suddenly."

"Yes, My Lady."

Caroline was loathe to force a confidence from her aunt's servant so she said no more on the subject. But she felt sure that she would have noticed any signs of weakness had her aunt suffered with a heart condition. Still, she could not be positive. The discussion of her attendance at the poetry reading was dropped and she sorrowfully wrote her note to Minnie declining the invitation.

Chapter 26

The Letters

Finally, August arrived and all the fashionable people were leaving London. The balls were over and Lady Culverwell and her daughter left London for their country home. The heat of August did not improve Miss Hilliard's temper and Lady Caroline suffered constantly with headache. One afternoon, when Miss Hilliard had been complaining of the heat, Lady Caroline ventured to suggest that they hasten their scheduled trip to the country.

"Think of the cool breezes that blow over the lake in the evening. How delicious it would be to be at Chilverton now."

"Yes, my dear, but your sister's confinement is soon. I do not want to be in the house during that event. It is all so unpleasant and the house will be in complete disorder."

"But, we might be of help to Julia and to Mama."

"We would just be in the way. I have no patience with all the fuss."

Lady Caroline was forced to give up her hopes and resigned herself to wait for another month to see her home and her family. But before August was completely over, she received a letter from her mother containing welcome news. It read as follows:

> "My Darling Caroline,
>
> You will be surprised to receive a letter from me so soon on the heels of my last, but I have the best of news to impart. Your brother and sister now have a daughter. Julia and the child are very well and the baby is the most darling little thing you have ever seen. I am writing this short note in hopes that you and your aunt will hasten your return to the country. I have also written to my sister to invite her to stay with me at the dower house if she wishes, and Hugh says you may have your old room.
>
> I shall be so excited to see you and to share all our joy with you. Do hurry down as soon as you can.
>
> Your ever loving and devoted Mama."

Lady Caroline could tell by her aunt's surprised exclamations that she had been reading her own letter from Lady Sylvia. "Oh, Aunt Clara! Such wonderful news!"

"Yes, apparently it has arrived. And Lady Julia is well; that is good news. I suppose you will be wanting to dash down to Chilverton immediately."

"Please, could we go now? I so want to be with them at this time. Do let us go as soon as possible, Aunt."

"We shall go but you must be patient. Nothing has been prepared for the journey."

"Oh, Aunt, I can be ready in two hours!"

"Do not be ridiculous, child! We can hardly leave by next week."

"But it has been so hot, Aunt Clara. Did you not say you would be glad to get out of the city?"

"That is so, my dear, and we will go as soon we can manage it. But the work will go slowly in this suffocating heat."

Lady Caroline, once she was able to retire to her room, sat down to re-read her letter. There was something in the mention of her room at home that disturbed her. Her mother had said that Hugh had given his permission for her to use her old room. This did not sound like she had been expected to return to that room permanently. The more she thought on it, the more she became convinced that she was not expected to stay with her family when her aunt returned to London. It was probable that Aunt Hilliard had written her mother to say that she would continue to live with her aunt in town, though she had never given her assent to this. Caroline strove hard to keep down the anger that was beginning to rise in her mind. She could not be sure that her aunt had written any such letter, but she strongly suspected it.

At tea that afternoon she questioned her aunt about her conjectures. "Aunt Clara, Mama does not appear to expect me to stay with her after our visit."

"Of course not, my dear. You will be returning with me to London. Your Mama knows all about it."

Lady Caroline's color heightened. "I did not know about it. Have you written to my mother to say so without discussing it with me?"

"It was discussed."

"I do not recall discussing it."

"Of course it was discussed. I remember you said that you did not wish to be an expense to me and I told you that it would not be a problem."

"But I never agreed to stay here beyond the Season."

"It is all arranged now. You are to stay in London with me."

"It cannot be arranged! I did not agree to stay. Aunt Clara, I cannot stay with you always."

"Cannot! And why can you not, ungrateful girl? Your Mama wishes it. Your brother wishes it."

"I cannot believe that they wish it."

"Do you doubt my word, girl?"

"No, but they would not say that they wished me to stay if they knew I did not wish it. And, I do not wish to stay."

"And why should you not wish it, I'd like to know? Have you not had balls and clothes and everything a girl could want?"

"You have been very generous, Aunt. You have provided everything but that which I really need: my home and the company of my family."

"Don't make such a fuss, child. You are to stay here and that is an end of it," said Miss Hilliard who then stormed out of the room.

For the first time in her life, Lady Caroline felt a strong, deep anger. Her face was burning with it. She was determined that she would not allow her aunt to direct her life as she was evidently resolved to do. The things that Sir Erskine had said to her echoed in her mind. Her aunt would never stop until she obtained her object. She would attack Lady Sylvia until she got the authority she wanted to keep Caroline with her. The only protection possible would be marriage. Lady Caroline went to her room and got out her writing implements. She would commit herself. She wrote a hurried note to Sir Erskine Wald agreeing to become his wife and asking him to call upon her as soon as possible.

Chapter 27

Lady Caroline's Decision

The next morning, Sir Erskine was with her early. "So, you have decided?" he asked.

"Yes," said Caroline with determination, "I have decided. I shall not let Aunt Hilliard take control of my very life. You were right. She intended to make me her permanent companion, and she would never have let me live at home in peace. She would have plagued my mother until she agreed with her. She does not give up when she has an end in mind."

"I think you are doing the right thing. And, I must say, it is a great help to me as well. My mother has been quite insistent on my getting married since I have come into the title. We shall make the ideal marriage!"

"Yes, my dear," said Lady Caroline, offering her cheek for a kiss, "I think we shall."

"Shall we inform the old octopus?"

"Yes, let's."

Miss Hilliard, surprised at such an early visit, and incensed at Lady Caroline being asked for instead of herself, came bustling into the drawing room as soon as she heard that Sir Erskine was in the house. "Sir Erskine, how early you are! I'm afraid you caught me unready. How are you this morning?"

"I am extremely well, Miss Hilliard, since I have the exquisite pleasure of informing you of my engagement to marry your niece."

Miss Hilliard staggered back. "Marry my niece! I am surprised at you, Sir Erskine. How long has this been going on behind my back?"

"Lady Caroline and I have been good friends for a long time," replied Sir Erskine. "I am sure we will have the complete approval of her brother."

"Not if I have anything to say about it! I hate this sort of underhand thing."

"I believe you have been present at all but one of my calls, Miss Hilliard. I made my proposal to Lady Caroline some months ago and this morning she has done me the honor to accept. I shall go immediately to Chilverton and speak to her brother."

"She has said nothing to me of any proposal."

"I saw no reason to trouble you, Aunt," said Lady Caroline. "I did not intend to accept the proposal until yesterday evening when I changed my mind."

"I see what you are about, little Miss!"

"There is nothing mysterious about it. Sir Erskine has made me a very generous offer and I have accepted him."

"We shall see about that. I shall write to your mother immediately."

"That is a very good idea. I shall write to her as well." Lady Caroline turned to Sir Erskine as Miss Hilliard flew out of the room. "Do you mean to go to Chilverton now?"

"Yes, I can leave immediately."

"Let me write but a short note to my mother that you may carry with you."

"Yes, of course."

Lady Caroline ran to her room and scribbled a note to tell her mother of her engagement and asking for her blessing. She apologized for the suddenness of the news and shortness of the note, saying that she would see her mother within the week. She went back to the drawing room and gave Sir Erskine the note. "I hope you do not repent of your bargain," she said.

"Not for the world! I am delighted with our plan. Now I shall ride forth like the wind to precede the ill wind of Miss Hilliard's missive."

"Give everyone my love."

"They shall have it." He squeezed her hand once and departed.

Lady Caroline watched Sir Erskine ride away and then returned to her room to begin packing. But she sat down on her little wooden chair instead of setting about her work right away and thought about what she had done. She asked herself if she had done well. She thought it all through again and again but there was only the one conclusion. There was nothing else she could do. She had no regrets. She could even look forward to her new life as she thought on all its advantages. Lady Caroline then called her maid and gave her instructions for the packing. As she worked she realized that she was quite happy for the first time in a very long while.

Chapter 28

The return to Chilverton

Within a few days the ladies had packed and were ready for the trip to Chilverton Park. Lady Caroline's excitement carried her through the fatigue of the drive and her aunt's icy ill will. As they drew near Chilverton, she sat eagerly forward, looking for every familiar sight and anticipating the first view of her beloved home. She knew that the effort and the excitement would take its toll on her the next day, but she could not restrain her emotion. When they arrived, Lady Sylvia met them in the hall. Lady Caroline flew into her mother's arms and burst into tears. Lord Hugh walked downstairs to greet his sister and aunt, then they all walked up to the drawing room where Lady Julia awaited their arrival. Soon the nurse brought the baby in to meet her aunt. Lady Caroline was entranced. The child was unusually beautiful, with long tapered fingers and large intelligent eyes.

"She is amazingly beautiful!" said Lady Caroline. "Oh, Hugh, Julia, she is so perfect!"

"We think so," said Lord Hugh. Lady Julia was beaming.

"Her name will be Sylvia Elizabeth Marie."

"It looks very well," remarked Aunt Clara stiffly. "I can see the Hilliard countenance in it."

Lady Caroline turned to her mother. "Mama, I am a little fatigued after our journey."

"Quite naturally so, my dear. Julia will understand if you wish to rest for a while. I will walk up to the room with you."

Once in her room, Lady Caroline turned to her mother. "Mama, I suppose you were surprised at my note."

"I was surprised, dear, but so pleased as well. Sir Erskine is a fine young man." She hugged her daughter.

"I'm pleased too, Mama."

"But I suppose my sister is sorry to lose you."

"She does not approve of our engagement, but she gives no reason for her disapprobation."

"In her letter to me she said that it had been done in an underhand way."

Lady Caroline colored. "She says that, but she was present at every visit of Sir Erskine's except the one when he made his proposal."

"I suppose she wished he had asked her permission before he spoke to you."

"She had encouraged his visits. Neither of us thought she would have an objection."

"Well, you know that your aunt likes to be consulted. I suppose she is merely sorry to lose your company since you had previously agreed to live with her."

"That is something that was never true. I never agreed to live with her. She cannot truthfully say that I did."

"Well, dear, that is all past now that you are engaged. And, I must say, I am glad to have you settled so close to us here and not in London."

"Oh, I am too, Mama! I never liked London. I shall be so happy here."

"You shall have your own home now."

"Yes, that is what I mean. But I shall be at Chilverton as often as I can."

"Get some rest, now, Darling. It is so good to have you at home!"

The next morning Lord Hugh asked his sister to come to him in his library.

"I've had a visit from Sir Erskine Wald. Is this all true, Caroline? Do you really want to marry the man?"

"Yes, Hugh, I do. I have thought much about it, and I have decided that it is the best thing I can do."

"I can't but believe that you are throwing yourself away in this."

"Hugh, please listen to me. It is not throwing myself away if my health is so poor that I cannot have children. What other man shall I marry who would not wish for an heir?"

"But why need you marry at all, if that is the case?"

"I want my own home. I want to live as close as possible to Chilverton and not in London. I want my mother to be free of pressure from my Aunt Hilliard. Hugh, you know that when Aunt Hilliard has an object in view, she cannot be stopped. She will have no mercy on my mother until she has secured me as her permanent companion in London. It is only if I am protected by the authority of a husband that she will accept defeat."

"Perhaps you are right."

"You know I am right, Hugh."

"Are you quite sure that Sir Erskine will be all that you expect? You do realize that he will still spend most of his time in London."

"I know that Sir Erskine does not expect to change his life for me. But what he offers me is all I need or expect from life: a home close to Chilverton, the protection of a husband, and congenial company from time to time. I do not suppose I shall find fulfillment in marriage as other women do. I expect to find my fulfillment in the whole family. I must warn you that you will find me here almost daily after my marriage."

That will be as we will like it." Lord Hugh smiled. "If you are positively sure that this is what you want, then I shall give you my blessing."

Lady Caroline kissed her brother fondly. "Thank you, Darling. It is what I want."

Caroline went to her room to write to Sir Erskine. On the way she encountered her aunt, who stiffened as she saw her. "You have been to see your brother. I suppose he has forbidden this nonsense of marriage."

"No, Aunt Clara. Hugh has seen fit to approve my engagement with Sir Erskine."

"We shall see about that." Miss Hilliard steamed toward Lord Hugh's library. She knocked and entered without waiting for an invitation. "What is this I hear? You surely do not approve this pretense of a marriage!"

"Come in, Aunt Clara" said Lord Hugh, wryly. "I certainly do approve of Caroline's engagement to Sir Erskine Wald."

"What? That must be nonsense! We would be the mockery of the county! The man is a confirmed bachelor!"

"Sir Erskine is a baronet and respected landowner in this county. Who would dare mock his marriage to the sister of the Earl of Chilverton?"

"You know very well of what I am speaking."

"There has been no scandal or calumny linked to Sir Erskine's name. I have known him very well all of my life and I will hear no word spoken against him."

"Very well, if you are determined to countenance this charade. But I warn you, no good can come of this marriage."

"I beg to disagree. I see now that a great deal of good will be accomplished by the marriage."

"Hmph! Well..!" Miss Hilliard, at an uncharacteristic loss for words, could only retreat from the room.

Chapter 29

The Engagement Is Announced

Though Lady Caroline's joy in her engagement was of a subdued nature, she was exceedingly thrilled to anticipate complete freedom from her Aunt Hilliard's intrusions. She sought her sister Julia in the drawing room and found her caressing little Sylvia Elizabeth, with Nurse standing by dotingly.

"Oh, here is my sweet little niece! May I hold her, Julia?"

"Of course you may. I hope she will be your little darling as she is mine."

"She is that already. Such a sweet little face..."

The sisters cooed and exclaimed over the perfections of the child until Nurse took her up for her nap.

"Julia, let me tell you my news. I am engaged to be married to Sir Erskine Wald. Hugh has just given us his blessing."

Lady Julia kissed her sister. "Oh Caroline! That is such good news. I do wish you joy!"

"Have you met Sir Erskine?"

"I have not. I was aware that he was in the house to see Hugh last week, but he did not stay."

"I hope you will love him."

"I shall certainly love him for your sake. Tell me of him. Hugh says he was a childhood friend."

"Yes, we were all great friends as children. He has been my best friend through everything. He understands me better than anyone."

"That is so important in marriage."

Lady Sylvia entered the drawing room. "I have just spoken with Hugh, Caroline dear, and I am so pleased that he has given his approval." She kissed her daughter.

"Thank you, Mama."

At that moment the door opened to admit Miss Hilliard. She stood a moment and glared at the happy trio, and then said with a look of stern determination, "Sylvia, I wish to speak with you. In private."

"Certainly, Clara." Lady Sylvia exchanged a look of understanding with her daughter as she left the room with her sister.

"You have heard, I suppose, that Lord Hugh has given his approval to this absurd engagement," began Miss Hilliard when she and Lady Sylvia were alone.

"Yes, and I have done so as well," responded her sister stoutly.

"Then you must take it back again! This engagement is a travesty and not to be permitted."

"What evil do you suspect of Sir Erskine, sister, that you use such strong language. I cannot suppose you mean anything by it."

"I do! I mean that Sir Erskine Wald has never been considered a marrying man, and yet this parody of a marriage is proposed. Do you really mean to link your daughter's name with such a man?"

"I have known Sir Erskine since he was a boy. His mother is a dear friend of mine as well as yours. He has always been a gentleman and has done well for himself. How can you say such things of him? I know nothing against him, nor do you, I suppose. Have you any specific accusations to make?"

"Well, not at the moment. But I am sure that things are not right with him. His name has never been mentioned with another lady's."

"It is usually considered a good thing that there are no other attachments."

"You know what I mean, Sylvia."

"Yes, I do. And, I consider it very ill-natured of you to bring it up. I hope that you will speak of this no more. I shall be extremely affronted if you do speak of such things to anyone else."

Miss Hilliard puffed in exasperation. She had not expected her sister to stand up to her with such courage. "Very well, Sylvia. But remember what I have said. There shall be no good to come of this marriage." Miss Hilliard marched to her room in dudgeon and stayed there for the rest of the day considering her situation. She did not like to show herself defeated among her family. But fume and plot as she might, she could think of no further action to take against her niece presently, for fear of Lord Hugh.

At tea, Mrs. Pettigrew arrived to pay her respects to Lady Caroline. Miss Hilliard decided to leave her room for the occasion.

"We have such happy news to tell you, Mrs. Pettigrew," said Lady Sylvia, "and you will be the first outside the family to know it. Lady Caroline is engaged to be married to our dear friend, Sir Erskine Wald."

"Happy news indeed! Let me wish you joy, Lady Caroline. I am so pleased for you."

"Thank you so much Mrs. Pettigrew. I am very pleased myself."

Miss Hilliard looked on with a dour expression. The rest of the ladies talked on with excitement in which she could not join. Her temper was strained to the breaking point. She stood suddenly and declared that she had a headache and would go to her room.

The next morning Miss Hilliard announced to her sister that she would be leaving immediately for London as she could not enter into the festive atmosphere then prevailing at Chilverton.

Chapter 30

A Date Is Set

Within a few days Sir Erskine arrived. Lord Hugh had written to give his approval to the engagement and had invited him to join the family at Chilverton. He received a hearty welcome from Lord Hugh and greeted Lady Caroline with both hands. She felt such gratitude for him that she almost felt that she was in love with him. "How is your mother?" she asked later as they were walking on the lawn.

"My mother is ecstatic," he replied. "She cannot yet contain her joy."

"Dear Mrs. Wald."

"You must call her Mama now."

"How nice that will be."

"I suppose your aunt cut up rough."

"Oh, heavens! I have never seen her so furious. She did everything she could to sway my mother against our engagement. I am so proud of Mama; she stood firm with us."

"As will my mother. Miss Hilliard shall find a stout opponent in Mother should she decide to cross blades with her."

Lady Caroline laughed delightedly at the image of her aunt contending with the formidable Mrs. Wald. "I believe that my aunt would lack the courage to fence with your mother."

"Tell me, my dear, when shall we set our date?" asked Sir Erskine.

"I do not have an idea. Have you thought about it? I don't suppose there is any hurry."

"I think it would be well to get you established in your home."

"That does sound appealing. I do not want to impose on Hugh any longer than necessary. I shall move to the dower house soon and remain there until we are married."

"That may not be necessary. How much time do we need before the ceremony?"

"I suppose three months is considered the minimum of time needed for the preparations."

"Then I suppose we shall make another Christmas Wedding. But Caroline, I do not want you to wear out your health. Perhaps it will be better to take more time. Let us say March or April."

"Perhaps you are right. I have been riding on a cloud of excitement that will dissipate soon. I must remember to pace myself as usual."

"I should say that is absolutely necessary. I do not want my bride-to-be overtaxed. There is no rush now that your Aunt Hilliard has been put in her place."

"My Aunt Hilliard has a way of not staying in her place. But I do not think that she can interfere with me now. At least I hope not."

"I cannot think of anything she could do. Not if your brother and Mama stay with us."

"I must admit I am still afraid of her. I cannot imagine my life truly free from her influence. She knows she can strike me by attacking my mother."

"What can she do that she has not already tried?"

"She can continually criticize us and plague Mama about the prospect of a childless marriage."

"Does your mother not agree with you that you must not bear children?"

"She does, but I believe that she has held out some hope in her heart. Aunt Clara can cause her much pain on that point and I have no doubt she will."

"I must find a way to stop her malice. It is incomprehensible!"

"Oh, if we could only do so! Dear Erskine, if you could do that for me I should be more grateful than I can say!"

"I shall devote my entire attention to it, my dear. My mother may be of some help to us in this. You will see, we shall do everything possible to keep your aunt within bounds. She will not distress your mama if I can prevent it."

Chapter 31

A Visit to Mrs. Wald

Mrs. Hortensia Wald bustled with her typical energy into the breakfast room at her house in London where she found her son, Sir Erskine, dawdling over his toast. "You are early, my dear."

"I have been thinking, Mother. Perhaps you may have some idea how we may be of help to Lady Caroline."

"What sort of help do you mean?"

"You are, of course, very well acquainted with her aunt, Miss Clara Hilliard?"

"Very well indeed."

"So you are aware of the kind of opposition she can pose when she has her back up?"

"I see! Clara is making herself unpleasant, is she?"

"She is. And she knows how to do it." Erskine poured out tea for his mother. "She has opposed our engagement rather strenuously and Caroline is concerned that she may go further still."

"In what way?"

"You are aware that she does not believe Caroline to have been ill at all during these past few years. That is how she got in trouble with old Lord Harold."

"Yes, she overstepped there rather badly."

"You may know that Caroline and I do not plan to have children. I have no desire for them and Caro is too weak to attempt it."

"I suspected that some such arrangement had been made between you."

"Well, Miss Hilliard is attacking Lady Sylvia on that point. She puts the blame of it entirely on me since she believes Caroline to be in perfect health. If Lady Sylvia becomes convinced that she might still hope for grandchildren were Caroline to marry elsewhere, there might be trouble."

"Yes, I see your position."

"In addition to that," continued Sir Erskine, "I do not trust Miss Hilliard to refrain from talking of the matter outside of the family. Caroline feels that she is too afraid of Lord Hugh to start anything but I am not so assured of it."

"No indeed! Lord Hugh does not have eyes and ears in London to inform him of her activities. Therefore, we must provide them for him."

"Exactly! I knew I could count on you, Mother."

"Leave it to me, my boy." Mrs. Wald set her cup sharply on its saucer.

"Now, Lady Caroline has seen a doctor about her complaints, no doubt."

"She has seen many doctors over several years and none of them can find what is wrong."

"I think I shall be able to help you there. I know of a specialist who might be of service. Let me invite Lady Caroline to stay with me in London while she does her shopping. I think I may be able to convince her to see him."

"Do you think he will find anything more than the other specialists she has seen?"

"She has just not seen the right man. This doctor specializes in obscure ailments. I think that, though he may not find anything specific, he will surely give a general idea what is wrong."

"That at least would be helpful to Caro."

"You may count on me, my dear."

"I knew that I could."

Mrs. Wald sat at her desk in her study and considered her plans. First, she wrote to Lady Caroline inviting her to visit her in London and do some shopping for her wedding clothes.

Then she went over in her mind a list of her friends who also knew Miss Clara Hilliard. There were two or three whom she knew she could trust. She made out a schedule of visits to these friends and crafted her plan of what she would say. To the friends she could trust to be discreet, she would tell her suspicions of Miss Hilliard. She would ask them to watch Miss Hilliard through all of their mutual acquaintance to see if Miss Hilliard would speak ill of the engagement. The rest of the friends she herself would visit regularly to see if any hint of such gossip appeared. If Miss Hilliard breathed a word of disapprobation of the engagement, Mrs. Wald should hear of it.

Having accepted Mrs. Wald's invitation to visit, Lady Caroline arrived in London prepared to do some shopping. The excitement surrounding her engagement had taken its toll on her and the trip fatigued her more than she expected. Mrs. Wald was all sympathy. "My dear, you must go to your room this minute and lie down. You must be worn through."

"How kind you are, Mrs. Wald. Yes, I am somewhat fatigued by the journey."

"Come, let me take you upstairs. How has your health been, my dear? Erskine has said that the excitement may have been too much for you."

"Yes, I fear I have outdone my strength. I hope you will not think it rude of me if I rest a day or two."

"Not at all, dear girl. I expected that you should need some time. Shall I have some tea brought up for you?"

"Oh, yes, thank you. Some tea would be wonderful."

Mrs. Wald was patient until Lady Caroline felt stronger and was able to come down the next day. "Are you feeling better, my dear?"

"I think I will be fine now, thank you. It was so good of you to let me rest."

"Not at all. I have been thinking about your health, dear Lady Caroline. I have been very concerned about you. Erskine has told me that you have seen many doctors and none were able to help you. Let me tell you of a specialist, whom I wish you would see, who may be able to understand your condition."

"I wish that he might but I have been to see so many doctors with no results."

"I know my dear, but this Dr. Manning is different. He is aware that there are complaints that the medical science has not yet defined. He takes the patient's whole life into account and will ask you many questions that the other doctors do not. I have even heard it said that he encourages the patient to write out a history of his illness and list every symptom he experiences, however minor."

"That does sound different. Oh, if he could only tell me what is wrong!"

"If anyone can, I believe that this is the man. Would you like to see him?"

Lady Caroline considered it, and replied, "I will if you think I should."

"I shall write to him this very evening."

A few days later, Doctor Cornelius Manning called and spoke with Lady Caroline for a very long time. He asked her about her childhood and the places she had visited about the time she became ill. Never had a doctor examined her in such detail and with such interest and respect. When he was ready to give his opinion, he sat face to face with her and spoke kindly to her. "Lady Caroline, I believe that you have been exposed to a malignant bacterium called borrelia during your time in Scotland some years ago. It is not a matter that can be proven and the diagnosis is not a widely accepted one, but all the symptoms are there. The illness has left you weakened and has affected your heart. In my opinion, you should not attempt to bear a child. I do not think your heart is strong enough for childbirth. If you did survive, your weakness would be much exacerbated. I wish I could offer you a cure, but there is none known. I can, however, prescribe you some fortifying tonics to help you gain some strength." Mrs. Wald took the prescriptions and saw the doctor out.

Lady Caroline was deeply grateful to at last have a doctor take her complaints seriously and to have an opinion that explained her weakness. But to hear her fate pronounced so clearly affected her sadly and she had to resort to tears. Mrs. Wald was instantly by her side. "There, my dear. It is only what we expected, is it not? And perhaps the tonics will be of some help."

"I am sorry, Mrs. Wald. It is just that it is so good to finally know what is wrong with me and to be listened to and believed. You cannot know what a relief it is!"

"I know, my darling, I know. And your Mama will be relieved too, will she not, to know that we finally have a firm opinion?"

"Oh, Mama! I must write to her."

"And I will write too, dear."

Chapter 32

Mrs. Wald Is Equal to the Task

Christmas had passed and the preparations for Lady Caroline's wedding were progressing well. Sir Erskine had spent quite some time during the holiday at Chilverton, and had presented Lady Caroline with an elegant ruby and diamond ring. Miss Hilliard had not visited the family at Christmas, saying that she owed a visit to an old friend in Bath. She had been mostly silent on the subject of Caroline's engagement since she had left Chilverton in September, giving her sister to know that she was offended. Still, it was not like Miss Hilliard to accept defeat easily.

One morning in February Miss Hilliard received a call from her friend, Mrs. Pettigrew, who was in London for a few days of shopping. Mrs. Pettigrew was full of news from Chilverton about Lady Caroline's wedding preparations. It was finally too much for Miss Hilliard and her malice escaped her. "Don't talk to me of that wretched wedding!" she said. "There will be no good to come of it, I assure you."

"Why, whatever do you mean, Clara?"

"I mean that there will be no children produced by that union. Sir Erskine Wald has been a confirmed bachelor all his life. I do not believe that a leopard changes his spots!"

Mrs. Pettigrew was shocked into silence. She could hardly wait to escape Miss Hilliard's drawing room to go to her friends and ask their opinion of this speech. Fortunately, the friend with whom she chose to share this new information was a certain Mrs. Willingham, a dear and trusted friend of Mrs. Wald. Mrs. Willingham gave Mrs. Pettigrew the sage advice to let the calumny go no further. "I can tell you, dear Mrs. Pettigrew, that Sir Erskine Wald and his mother have been my acquaintances for a great many years and there has never been such a thing said about him. He is a gentleman and a baronet and Miss Hilliard would do well to keep her unfounded opinions to herself."

Directly upon Mrs. Pettigrew's departure, Mrs. Willingham took herself to call upon her friend, Mrs. Hortensia Wald. "You were quite right, my dear," said Mrs. Willingham. "Miss Hilliard was not able to keep silence. She has said her piece to Mrs. Pettigrew, though I think I quashed it there."

"What did she say?"

Mrs. Willingham reported the conversation as it had been told to her.

"I thought as much. I shall have to pay a visit to our dear Miss Hilliard," said Mrs. Wald with a look that boded no good to Miss Hilliard.

The very next morning Mrs. Wald was at Miss Hilliard's doorstep. Miss Hilliard was surprised and somewhat conscious of her remarks of the previous day. "Hortensia, my dear, what an age it has been since I have seen you."

"It has been indeed, Clara. Too long! I thought I would just drop in to bring you the latest news of our dear Lady Caroline."

"News?" inquired Miss Hilliard nervously.

"Yes, so sad. She has seen the very distinguished specialist, Dr. Cornelius Manning, and his opinion was very grave. It seems that Lady Caroline's heart is weakened and she will not be able to hope for children.

Miss Hilliard colored.

"I know this is a shock to you, Clara, and I am sorry to be the bearer of bad news. But we must all bear up for dear Lady Caroline's sake and give her our support."

"Of course," said Miss Hilliard.

"People will talk, you know. There is always someone ill-natured enough to carry a tale, but we must stand together. May I count on you to contradict any gossip you may hear?" Mrs. Wald gave Miss Hilliard one of her terrifying smiles.

"Count on me?" murmured Miss Hilliard nervously, "Yes, of course."

"I knew I should. You see, I could not stand by and let the young people be made unhappy by any spiteful tittle-tattle that may result from her unfortunate condition."

Miss Hilliard turned beet red.

"I am so glad you understand me, my dear."

Chapter 33

Wald Abbey

Early in April, the day of the wedding came to find Chilverton full of the usual bustle and excitement that accompanies such a happy event. Lady Sylvia had taken great care to insure that Lady Caroline did not overly exert herself. Lord Hugh and Lady Julia had given the wedding breakfast, which had gone off beautifully. Lady Caroline, who had chosen the simplest but most elegant of gowns, looked the very picture of a lovely bride. After the wedding, the couple left Chilverton for a long honeymoon in Bath, where Sir Erskine had taken some fashionable rooms, very convenient to the pump room. Lady Caroline had an interest in taking the waters to see if they might have a salubrious effect similar to the strengthening tonics the doctor had prescribed.

Miss Hilliard had not attended the wedding, saying that she never liked weddings, which was true, and that she felt she needed a rest, which was quite obviously not true. She had meant to snub her niece and her sister, but would have been furious to learn that they were only relieved that she was not to come. She had, however sent what she intended to be a generous wedding gift, a very elaborate and expensive vase, which Lady Caroline could never bring herself to like.

The honeymooners returned from Bath to take up residence at Wald Abbey, after stopping first in London to stay a day or two with Mrs. Wald. Though much smaller than Chilverton, Wald Abbey was comfortable and situated on a hill with lovely surrounding countryside. It had been occupied by the bachelor, Sir John, for so many years that it needed a woman's touch to bring its rooms back to life. Sir Erskine and Lady Caroline had entered into this endeavor with much delight and good taste during their engagement so that the house was ready to receive them on their return. Lady Caroline felt like she was coming home.

"Oh, Erskine, look! The drawing room has turned out beautifully! You were so right about the chairs; they are elegant."

"Yes, I am an adept when it comes to chairs."

"The piano is perfect in that spot."

"It is tempting us to play a duet." Sir Erskine arranged the music and the couple sat down to play one of their favorites. They enjoyed several happy moments of music until Lady Caroline became fatigued. "I am sorry, Erskine, I cannot finish."

"Perhaps you should rest for a while. Let me take you to your room. I hope Mrs. Wren has had it properly prepared for you."

"Irises! Mrs. Wren has brought some flowers in for me. How nice," exclaimed Lady Caroline upon entering her room. "Oh, Erskine, I'm so happy. You have given me everything I could possibly want and I am so grateful to you."

"Don't be grateful, my dear. It has been only exactly what I wanted as well, and entirely my pleasure. Now you have a good rest. I shall see you at tea."

Lady Caroline woke from a long rest and sat up in her new bed. *What a lovely room this is*, she thought. *I can hardly believe it is my room, but there is my writing desk and my mirror.* She dressed herself and went down to the drawing room.

"How nice this is, sitting down to tea like an old married couple."

Sir Erskine laughed. "I hope we may grow to be an old married couple together."

"As do I." Lady Caroline smiled affectionately and sipped her tea. "I think I should like the carriage tomorrow to go to see Mama. It is her birthday soon."

"My dear, the carriage is there for you. You must take it out at any time you please and not ask my permission. And, if Mama's birthday is soon, let us have a dinner for her here."

"And we shall have your Mama here too! That will make a nice little party, along with Hugh and Julia, of course."

What an excellent idea! The very thing to do!"

Lady Caroline soon busied herself with preparations for the dinner party with the help of Mrs. Wren, the housekeeper. Before the day for the party arrived, some discomfiting news arrived from Chilverton Cottage. Miss Hilliard had made a surprise visit and Lady Sylvia asked if she might bring her sister to the dinner. Lady Caroline agreed and extended an invitation to her aunt, but she feared that Miss Hilliard's presence would bring a chill to the party.

The evening of the dinner party arrived and Sir Erskine and Lady Caroline received their guests in their newly refurbished drawing room. Lady Sylvia, Lady Julia and Mrs. Wald were all charmed at the changes that had been made to the rooms. All the chintzes and chairs were exclaimed over with delight. Miss Hilliard looked at everything without uttering a sound.

At dinner Lord Hugh made an announcement: "Julia and I are expecting a new addition to the family!"

"Another one!" exclaimed Miss Hilliard, apparently aghast. Then she corrected herself. "How wonderful!"

The festive air of the party was much improved by the announcement of the new baby and everyone celebrated the excellent news. By the end of the evening, even Miss Hilliard seemed to be enjoying herself. As the company took their leave she kissed her niece and said, "I must admit you have done well for yourself. The Abbey is a beautiful home."

"Thank you, Aunt," said Lady Caroline. "I hope you will visit us again."

The old lady seemed mollified. "Perhaps I shall, if you will have me."

"We should be delighted."

Sir Erskine smiled as he recognized Miss Hilliard's final admission of defeat.

Printed in the United States
By Bookmasters